ETERNAL LOVE

ETERNAL

LOVE

Karimah Colden

DEDICATION

I finally did it! Book two in the Eternal Series is done, and I have so many to thank for supporting (and advocating for) me throughout this entire process.   I don't think I have ever pushed myself so hard in my life, and I am truly proud of the end result. Eternal Love has been a labor of love.

To my cousins Rae, Rashon, Fonnie & May, Eric & Kathy, Dina, Jeff & Tahese, & Mendela. Not only did you show support for my first project, but you pushed me through the second. I felt so much love from ya'll that no amount of *thank yous* could do you justice. My sisters from another Mister: Nadiyah, Akila, Jessica, Tiffany, Tashena, Kiara & MJ. Thank you so much for putting up with the many text, emails, messages & calls during random times of the day & not killing me. To the guys in my life that exceeded every expectation of what a friend should be. Mario, Kody, Durant, Demarcus, Demarius, Rich, Will, Roger & Ben. Not only do ya'll have my back in life, but you support my dream & have never doubted my vision or talent. To my Towers High Alumni, thank you for showing the world how Titans do!…& a special thank you to my fellow Titans Lucretia & Jeff, who made sure to purchase my first book, your support is forever appreciated. This would not be complete without mentioning a few more people that I am so blessed & thankful for who have also shown so much support and faith in my work: Annazette, Ebony, Aunt Gail, Aunt Gerrie, Jennifer, Mrs. Jeanette, Jen, Nina, Donna, Valerie, Esther, Kelly, Alison, Michelle, Nikki. Thank you to Tia and the Ladies at Love Hair Salon for opening your doors to me; to my Astor family (including Alvin, Mr. Pruitt, Dee-Bloo, Carrie, Evelyn, Jeff, Melissa & Melissa, Joslyn, & Michelle) for not hesitating to embrace & show so much love for my work. To my Pastor, Doris Schuyler & my family at Riverview Missionary Baptist Church (with a huge thank you to Mother Ida). It's near impossible for me to express my gratitude for the unending support that you shower upon me daily. I am eternally & exceedingly grateful. Last but not least, thank you to the first bookstore to accept my work. You gave a home to me & so many other independent authors & I am so thankful for your vision: Mahogany Reads Café. May you continue to grow & prosper. If you don't see your name, please don't think that I've forgotten about you. I still have two more books to go so & many more thank-yous to give!

Prologue

Bayou Pierre, Red River Parish, Louisiana-1925

"Nic, she's gone. Nokin mé mouri, li gònn," Tempest cried heavily into her sister's shoulder.

"Please be strong mô soer. We will get through this, I promise," Nicola replied, comforting her younger sibling.

Christophe-Jerard stood in the doorway of their wetland home staring at his twin daughters as they grieved for their mother. It had only been a few days since Aiyana took her last breath as she gave birth to their stillborn son, but Cristophe-Jerard had yet to shed a tear.

"C.J., it is time," the old priest said solemnly, joining his companion in the doorway. "Would you like me to bring the girls?"

"Sivouplé non, give them a moment. We will be there," he answered, resting his hand reassuringly on the kindly man's shoulder.

As unfeeling as C.J. was said to be, it did pain him to witness his daughters in such a state of heartache; but he knew, as with all things, time would allow the pain to pass.

The priest gave the girls one last glance before walking back outside and heading toward the moor where Aiyana and son lay waiting. He had known the Etienne's since the girls were three. So along with his own heavy heart, he could relate to the intense pain that they must have been experiencing.

"Nicola, Tempest...we must go," C.J. finally said to his teary-eyed daughters.

It was barely sunrise, but they had to begin their nearly eight-hour trip to New Orleans. This is where the Etienne mausoleum rested and awaited the bodies of his wife and son. C.J. decided to take the opportunity their passing presented and move him and the girls to New Orleans, as he had long wanted to do.

"Mô pé, do we have to leave?" Tempest asked with much sadness in her voice while they walked toward the beat-up truck. "We are taking mær to rest, but her spirit is here, I can still feel it."

C.J. did not want to share with the girls the reason for his plans just yet. But in recent years, he had witnessed their powers grow exceedingly. And with the passing of two so close in their bloodline, additional inherited powers would soon be shifting to them as well.

C.J. needed to bring the girls some place where he could grow their gifts as they hid in plain sight. Until they were properly trained they'd be open to much outside influence, and he couldn't allow their gifts to be tainted in that way.

"This is for the best," C.J. answered, "your mother will be with you wherever you go, just keep your heart open to her."

And just like that, they were loaded into the waiting vehicle along with the last of their belongings. As they looked back, the only home they'd ever known becoming smaller with distance, both girls felt a piece of them being ripped out. A void that, unbeknownst to either sister, would leave them confused, vulnerable and open to a lingering presence.

"It'll be okay Temp," Nicola said, leaning in nearer to her sister. "This is a chance to escape what we *should* have been, and become whatever we choose."

Plaquemines Parish, Louisiana-1927

"Tempest, you can't go on like this. Mær has been gone now for nearly two years, don't you think she would want you to live?" Nicola asked exasperatingly to her sister, who sat in the middle of their room chanting over an aromatic mixture of herbs and oils.

Nicola paced back and forth across the floor, growing more and more impatient with her twin. Since their mother died, Tempest had spent most days seeking out Aiyana's spirit and trying to communicate with her. Nicola and C.J. were tolerant in the beginning, but their father quickly grew weary of Tempest's tears and emotional breakdowns.

"Would you please answer me? Just say something so I know you're still in there," Nicola begged, falling to her knees and cupping her sister's face in her hands.

Looking up, Tempest's eyes were as bleak as when her mother's body had been sealed within her final resting place. Truth be told, it wasn't just missing her mother that caused Tempest to grieve so heavily; it was the surge in her natural abilities once their mother and brother had been properly committed to the earth.

The power was overwhelming, the voices were consuming and she could no longer tell the living from the deceased. Aiyana had been frequenting Tempest's dreams, warning her of something, but she couldn't hear her. She didn't dare share this with her father though; Tempest could sense his desire for power and control, and she did not like it.

"I'm still here Nic, I'm not going anywhere," Tempest answered her sister, standing up from the scorched copper bowl and walking to her bed. "I just need to rest for a little bit."

Nicola looked down at her sister, then pulled the covers over her. Tempest was the twin that looked most like their beautiful mother, and had so much of her spirit as well. She always had a gentleness about her that could be seen in her clear rainwater grey colored eyes. Tempest was also a healer, and refused to be sparing in her gifts. She freely made herb blends and medicinal brews for those less fortunate whenever she managed to avoid the ever-watchful gaze of her father.

After her sister drifted off, Nicola went to find C.J. Most of the time she felt like all he saw was power when he looked at his fifteen-year-old daughters. Their natural abilities far exceeded his own, as well as anything that could be taught. But Nicola always dismissed that suspicion since it felt more like borderline blasphemy. After all, C.J. was their father and he *had* to love them unconditionally…right? So, when he'd instructed Nicola to report her sister's doings and health, she was sure that it was only because he was so protective over them.

"Pær!" Nicola called out walking into the sitting room of their New Orleans home. "Pær, where are you?"

"You don't have to keep such noise, you'll wake the dead," C.J. said from the kitchen table where he sat drinking a piping hot cup of lavender tea.

"I'm sorry father, but it's Tempest," Nicola replied, sitting down next to him. "Something is wrong."

"Mô piti," he said, looking into his daughter's amethyst eyes, "I fear she has a weak spirit like your mother."

Nicola was taken aback by her father's seemingly harsh words.

"How could you say that? How could you say something so unkind?!"

"Because it is true. This blood that you have from both me and your mother is very powerful; and of us, only I have been chosen to continue on. And soon of you and your sister, only you will be left, made to walk your existence without her."

The words C.J. spoke caused Nicola great distress. She loved her sister dearly and couldn't bear the thought of anything happening to, let alone having to live without, her.

"Tempest and I are equal; she is just hurting and can't figure things out right now."

At that, C.J. held her face firmly in his hands and the next words that he spoke were said with a different tone. He sounded almost...cruel.

"She is not your equal, as your mother was not mine. I loved her yes, but I could never put her above my own greatness. And now I have you, who will one day be the *last* one standing. This was never meant for two, only one."

Nicola could literally feel the energy radiating from her father's hands. There was a tingle, similar to a jolt of electricity. The sensation it gave her was almost euphoric, and was instantly addictive.

"What was that," she asked, as C.J. lowered his hands from her face.

"That is generations of powerful magick, natural magick, that was meant only for you. And when Tempest finally becomes consumed by her weaknesses, it will be that tenfold."

Nicola loved her twin sister with all of her heart, but could what her father just said be true? Could Tempest's grief be not only her undoing, but her sister's path to a power that intense? The thought had never crossed Nicola's mind before, to need or even want that much power. But as what she felt from her father's hands continued to course through her, she could not deny the rush that it gave.

Chapter 1

It had been close to two months since Reign had the vision of and was visited by her grandparents. She was still trying to wrap her head around all that had been learned. Reign had a difficult time grasping that, unbeknownst to her, her grandmother *had* loved so completely. Then to find out that someone had deliberately taken that love from Sophie by stealing her husband's life inflicted an almost unbearable pain.

Between the burden of knowing what happened to her grandfather and what he and Sophie were now expecting of her, Reign was at a loss. She had no idea where to begin or what to even looking for. Being deep in thought, she was startled when the phone rang.

"Hey Alexa, what's going on?" Reign answered absently, getting up and pacing the living room floor.

"I just wanted to check and make sure you were still okay for tonight. You've been a little distant lately and I'm really not trying to make a troubling situation worse."

"Lex, you are more than my best friend, you are my sister. Not *like* a sister, not play cousin, not buddy, not acquaintance…but *a sister.* I wouldn't miss your engagement party if the sky was raining enormous balls of fire and I left home without my nonflammable umbrella. This is major for you."

Reign knew that Alexa was concerned because Krystian was going to be there. It was a miracle that, in the week and a half after Alexa and Adrian had announced their engagement, she hadn't bumped into him once. But Reign had become a different person since ending things with him, or so she told herself. Physically she was stronger, and with the help of her father and the meditations, her magickal gifts were growing and evolving as well. But every time Krystian King crossed her mind, her stomach ended up in knots and her palms went sweaty. He was officially becoming the bane of her existence.

"I know I know," Alexa sighed into the phone, "I wish it didn't even have to be like this. You two were *so* happy together."

"Okay, see that right there. That was the border of the 'don't go there' territory and you just crossed the point of no return," Reign replied with a small hint of irritation. "Besides, I'm the very last person that you should be worrying about. What you need to be doing is getting prepared for this amazing engagement party that you magically and effortlessly pulled together in, what, a week?"

"Two weeks," Alexa laughed. "I love you Reign. I love you so much," she continued, her voice virtually dripping with the sentiment.

"I know hun, I love you too. Now please, get off the phone and go get yourself ready for tonight," Reign practically ordered her.

"Okay, I'll see you later."

Once she hung up the phone, Reign's irritation was apparent. Each day she'd spent a portion of her meditation time focusing on her need to forget about Krystian. She knew the logic sounded utterly ridiculous, but was desperate for any type of solace from her bruised heart.

For weeks, all Reign could think about were ways to take her rage out on him. But in the end she had to force herself be rational and see the truth. Yes, Krystian lied about (or omitted) almost everything from the very beginning; but he didn't purposely try to bring her harm. Unfortunately, this knowledge didn't take away from the fact that his lies and omissions had basically cost Reign her life and put her father's in jeopardy.

So now there were only four hours left to mentally and physically prepare herself for the second longest night in her life (the first being the initial time she and Krystian met). Reign headed to her closet and pulled out the black cocktail dress she'd bought the day before. And looking at the fabric that was meant to cling to her like a second skin, she allowed herself to admit her only goal that night: to become a distraction to the man who seemed to unintentionally, but incessantly, distract her.

As Reign stopped just within the banquet hall entrance, she could see the many curious eyes that glanced her way.

Some were in interest while others held excessive indecision. Reign preferred to keep her friendship circle small, so even though she recognized a lot of faces, she wasn't trying to cozy up to any of them if she didn't have to. Once Adrian and Alexa had been spotted, she continued in, her walk dripping with poise and confidence.

As Reign made her way intently toward her friends, she was oblivious when the heads of the other guests turned, admiring her in the black form fitting dress that complimented every curve of her body. The clingy material teasingly stopped an inch above her knees. Reign's bare arms were adorned with a delicate black sheer nylon fabric that also ran across the modest cut of the dresses cleavage. But if there was anything that could be described as scandalous that evening, it was the dangerously low plunge that was cut into the back of her dress, giving a peak to the two cute dimples in her lower back.

"I'm so glad you could make it," Alexa smiled as she hugged her. "I think the entire room is now in need of a triple bypass thanks to you," she whispered in Reign's ear before letting her go.

"Congratulations Adrian," Reign said, hugging him but still smiling from Alexa's comment.

"Thank you. I'm so glad you were able to make it. This celebration definitely couldn't have been complete without you," Adrian remarked.

"I wouldn't have missed it for anything in the world."

Alexa turned to Adrian and lovingly kissed him on the lips. Then, after locking her arm around Reign's, headed toward the bar.

"I just wanted you to know that Krystian is here. He showed up about ten minutes ago, stag and looking very much in the mood to socialize. I don't know where he wandered off to, so keep your cool," Alexa said discreetly as they sat at the bar.

"Has Lisa shown up yet?" Reign inquired, attempting to acknowledge Alexa's warning while remaining indifferent.

"Did you hear what I said?" Alexa asked, a little irritated by her seeming disregard.

Reign turned and looked at her. Without speaking, her facial expression said everything: *yes, I heard you. I knew he was going to be here. I am fine.*

Alexa didn't say another word, only nodded, then proceeded with their conversation.

"Yeah, she's here. I think she went to the...*hell*."

"She went to the *hell*?" Reign laughed.

"No, he's coming Reign. I see Krystian and he is headed this way," Alexa alerted her friend.

Refusing to give in to the intense urge to turn around, Reign placed her order upon being greeted by a handsome bartender with pointed interest. She remained composed, choosing not to let her indifferent façade fall simply because the man who'd been plaguing her thoughts for months was nearing her.

"Well, congratulations are in order," Krystian said once he reached them, then kissed Alexa on the cheek.

"It's so good to see you Krys. And thank you for coming, especially with such short notice.

"Now you know I wouldn't have missed this," he said with a smile.

Then the woman in the scandalous dress sitting next to Alexa drew his attention. He couldn't see her face, but something about her presence drew him.

"I'm being so rude. Alexa, you should introduce me to your friend while I order us a celebratory drink."

Reign kept her back to Krystian the entire time he spoke. Only after the bartender brought her drink did she turn. His initial expression at seeing Reign was worth the hour and a half it took to get dressed. And she successfully hid her smile as he stopped and absently gazed at her.

"I have one, but thank you anyway," Reign answered, taking a generous sip from her wine glass.

"Reign," he said with a slight pause. "Wow, it's really nice seeing you."

Krystian greeted her, but did not trust himself to allow any physical contact. The way she looked right now took him back to the first time they'd met. No matter what Reign looked like, she never failed to take his breath away.

"It's nice to see you too," she replied.

Inside, her anger was a blazing inferno, but outwardly she kept every emotion in check. Refusing to give in to her intensely conflicting emotions, she simply smiled and nodded politely.

It had been nearly two months since Krystian laid eyes on Reign. He had been keeping tabs on her and always knew where she was, but refused to be in a position where he had to actually be in her presence.

So now, in this moment, it was as though time stood still. With thick, curly hair draping invitingly over one shoulder, her scent engulfed him. It wasn't the usual jasmine and lavender she wore; this was heady, sensual, and quite literally radiated from her skin.

Alexa was sitting there watching the beginnings of an uncomfortable conversation when, out of the corner of her eye, she saw Lisa motion her to come over. Glancing back a Krystian, it appeared as though he wanted devour Reign, but was doing an amazing job controlling himself. Alexa knew she'd never hear the end of it, and as she stood up, Reign shot her a glare that would've killed a lesser person.

"I'll be right back. Adrian is over there talking to my father and I don't want him putting his foot in his mouth," Alexa said, excusing herself from the awkward moment.

Reign did not want to be left alone with Krystian, but there was no way she was going to run with her tail tucked between her legs.

"So, did you plan on sitting down?"

Krystian was surprised by how calm Reign seemed. If he'd realized anything during their times together, it was that this woman was fiercely loyal and expected the same of those around her. He was sure that, to her, he was a traitor. So why the polite gesture?

"Don't mind if I do," he answered, taking a chance and sliding into the seat next to her.

"Long island iced tea please," Reign said to the bartender when he came to take Krystian's order.

"You remembered," he replied with a grin.

The smile he flashed almost had Reign's palms going sweaty. She took another sip of wine before responding.

"Yeah. Some things you never forget, no matter how much you may want to."

"And yet and still, here we are," Krystian replied.

Alexa had made her way to Lisa, where they sat attempting to inconspicuously observe Reign and Krystian.

"Do you really think this is going to work?" Alexa asked.

"Well, between you and I, I bumped into Krystian a few weeks back. We had a conversation about why Reign suddenly can't stand to be in the same room with him," Lisa began. "And from everything that he told me, assuming it's all truth, there's no reason that, with the proper persuasion of course, she can't forgive him and move past it."

"Wait. So, you've been talking to Krystian *behind her back*?" Alexa asked with a puzzled expression. "You know Reign will kill you if she finds out," she continued without waiting for Lisa's reply.

"And that is exactly why she *isn't* going to find out," Lisa responded through clenched teeth. "Besides, talking to him has been very enlightening. Granted, he wasn't the most honest with her, he does care a great deal for Reign. I think he deserves a chance to fix his mess."

"What's going on over here," Adrian interjected, sitting at the table and joining the ladies.

It only took him a moment to realize that, even though they were trying to hide it, their attention was focused in a collective direction.

"Before you say anything," Alexa cut in, not giving him the chance to disapprove of their interference, "they haven't killed each other yet. Not to mention Reign is actually being quite cordial."

Adrian knew that his friend was probably very uncomfortable having to finally face Reign after avoiding her for so long. And though she was friendlier than expected, Krystian was no fool. He knew she wasn't going to make getting back into her good graces an easy task, but he would never walk away from her unless forced to do so.

"Wait, are they going to the dance floor," Lisa said with a grin.

Then they all continued to sit there, as if watching a top-rated soap opera.

"Why do I get the feeling that this is not going to end well," Alexa mumbled.

"So, you're sure you want to do this?" Reign asked as Krystian lead her to the nearly empty dance floor.

"Well, you haven't assaulted me with a steak knife yet, so I have to optimistically assume my odds of surviving a dance with you are favorable."

When they found a suitable spot on the floor, Krystian waited until Reign slid her arms around his neck before placing his hands on her waist. He was still not comfortable initiating any intimate contact between them.

"I've never seen you wear that before, but it fits you really well," he said, speaking of the black, silver and turquoise choker that was clasped snugly on her neck.

"Thank you," she replied, unsure of how to feel about him giving out compliments so freely. "My grandfather designed it for me."

"It suits you, especially the turquoise against your hair," Krystian said, continuing to admire the striking piece. "And I really am sorry about William. I know how much he meant to you," he added, with eyes full with sincerity.

Reign was a little uncomfortable with the casual talk about her grandfather, so she corrected him.

"Thank you. But I was talking about my mother's father."

Krystian was confused by her reference to her maternal grandfather. In all of their conversations she'd never mentioned him, and from everything he knew, Sophie died unwed. Fully aware that his right to probe her personal life ended months ago he went silent, but their rhythm remained unbroken.

As the slowly sensual dance continued, they stood extremely close and Reign couldn't help but to purposely look up at him. In the nearly three months that had passed, he looked as though he'd become even more striking. His features were so intense and defined, as if to lure in prey. Those eyes, lips and that damned smile, she'd never get him out of her head now.

"A penny for your thoughts," Krystian asked when she ended the lengthy stare.

"You should channel that inner upir for All Hollows," Reign began. "You have that broodingly intriguing look about you that would lure in girls like honey to a fly."

After a short pause, and grin, Krystian responded.

"That's all well and good, but I'm only attracted to women. And as it stands, I only want one woman."

His breath caught when she tilted her head down to hide the slight smile that crept up on her face. That, and the syncopated rhythm of their bodies, confirmed all he needed to know. Reign still cared for him, likely more than she would ever be inclined to admit. It was in that moment that he knew, no matter what, he would do everything possible to regain her trust. There was no way he could ever look at or feel for any woman the way he did Reign.

She must have had an idea where his thoughts were going because, in that instant, she stopped dancing.

"You know we can't do this."

"But we're not doing anything," Krystian replied almost pleadingly when she stepped out of his grasp.

"Yes we are Krystian. You lied to me..."

"I didn't lie to you," he said, interrupting her. But deep down he knew that she was right. *A lie by omission is still a lie*, he thought.

"Okay, so you didn't lie outright, but you kept secrets from me. Secrets that put me and everyone I love in danger. For crying out loud, your father wants me dead," Reign said, her tone deathly calm as she looked him in his eyes. "Wasn't there anything in you that thought it might be a good idea to share that?"

"Of course there was. But as I said, I would die before letting that happen," Krystian whispered just as low and close to her ear once he'd pulled her back to him. His face was only inches from hers and he could feel her rapid breaths on his neck.

All Reign had to do was give him the slightest gesture that she felt any of what he was feeling and he'd kiss her. He'd make up for all of the times that he regretted not doing so until she melted in his arms. It felt as though they were the only ones in the room while they stood there, consumed by one another, but both refusing to take the first step.

"I can't," Reign whispered with finality.

Sliding out of Krystian's embrace, she walked off to say goodnight to her friends. Then exited the banquet hall, desperate for the freeing night air.

Chapter 2

It had been three days since the evening of Adrian and Alexa's engagement party and Reign was trying desperately not to slip into old habits. She'd spent months occupying her time with training, the gallery, and meditations; but in less than four hours all of her efforts had gone to hell. Reign couldn't deny she still felt something for Krystian, but her plan would never work if she couldn't keep from melting every time he smiled or spoke her name.

The past couple months were unusually quiet considering all that had taken place. There were no ghosts or dreams, and she hadn't heard so much as a peep from Nicola. But Reign knew it wouldn't last long, so she continued to focus on her strategy.

"But how am I supposed to get any information from Krystian while at the same time keeping him distanced," she mumbled to herself as she sat lotus on her living room floor.

The candles flickered vibrantly, as if they knew what she was contemplating. Reign had intently remained focused on the Sahasrara, Anja, and Muladhara spirits in all of her meditations since she began doing them. Her desire had been to take the necessary steps toward walking into her full being; however, she was fearfully trapped within the familiar. Reign didn't want to admit it, but she was terrified of what the frequent and countless changes could bring into her life.

So many things had happened to her family in a very short period of time, and almost all of it could be traced back to Nicola. *Almost.* She couldn't leave out the very lucrative role that Donovan Tolliver played in all of this, and that was the reason it was so difficult for her to move past Krystian's mediocre betrayal. How different could things have been had he been up front with her in the beginning?

As she sat there, seemingly contemplating her entire existence, Reign's attention was drawn to her vibrating cell phone.

"Pær, it's so good to hear from you. Is everything ok?"

"Yes *Princesse*, everything is well," Julien responded.

"I'm sensing a but," Reign replied when her father hesitated a little too long for her liking.

"Unfortunately there is a but my love. Claudette came to me last night," he said, with slight reluctance as he spoke of Reign's long deceased mother. "This is the first time I've seen her since instructing me to send you those herbs after your grandfather passed."

Her Paw Paw was still a sore subject for Reign, especially since *he* hadn't visited her either. Amarré, Sophie, Hania-Kele...none of them came to her in dream or awake since she had become accepting her father's legacy.

"What did she say?" Reign asked.

"She said you are getting too comfortable. That you know what must be done, but yet you waver."

"She knows I can see her, why doesn't mær come to me. Why do I have to keep getting all of these messages through you?" Reign asked, not really expecting an answer, but wanting to voice her upset.

"She said you would question that," Julien conceded, taking another long pause before continuing. "If you see her, you may get too complacent. These things coming through me keeps the urgency real."

As disappointed as the explanation made her, Reign knew her father was right. She wanted to see Claudette because she missed her. Her mother wasn't going to her father for social reasons; it was to keep her daughter on task.

"So, did she say anything else?" Reign sighed.

"Yes. She said 'Vishuddha and Manipura wait'."

Claudette was referring to the chakra spirits that Reign had begun using as guides during meditation. Upon first starting, she only thought them points for her to focus on. But as she began to channel her life force deeper and deeper into the meditations, they revealed themselves to be actual spirits. Seven spirits that guided and strengthened her, allowing Reign to harness and direct the magick that had begun to overcome her. The only problem was that when she stopped at the first three, her magickal progression stopped as well.

"And there is something else," Julien continued, "something is not right."

"What do you mean?"

"I know just by the natural order that as *you* grow stronger, I will grow a little weaker. But I feel like my magick is being drawn out by something else, something darker."

At Julien's words, a chill went up Reign spine.

"Do you know what it could be?"

"Only blood could pull from me like this. I know your Paw Paw would never do such a thing, and besides that, his energy is not dark. I can only think it Nicola finally reemerging."

Reign shuddered at hearing her great grandmother's name. The threat of Nicola always remained real, but her lack of appearance caused Reign to grow content and dismissive. Her mother was right, she was getting too comfortable and that had to change.

"I was thinking, why don't you come and stay with me for a while? At least until all of this craziness blows over," Reign said, voicing what she had been feeling for some time.

"Do you not think I can take care of myself?" Julien asked, only feigning insult.

"No, it's not that. But something you said confirmed a thought I'd been having for a while. Our powers trickle down generationally, right?"

"Yes."

"Well, I don't think it's a huge secret that Nicola's goal is to come for me. But if she is trying to be some all-powerful risen corpse, she either has to kill you or take your magick first," Reign concluded, hating saying the words, but hoping her father agreed with her.

"Chér, I knew this. But I can't stay there and lead her right to you. You must continue to strengthen yourself without worry of what may, *or may not*, happen."

"She's going to come after me whether you are here or not," Reign replied, a little frustrated by her father's refusal of her offer. "We would be much stronger together than apart."

"Princesse, I would only serve as a distraction. You need to put all of your energy into growing your magick. You've turned a blind eye to it all your life, and now thirty-five years of abilities are flooding you like the Mississippi. Chér, I will be fine; you have not drawn so much of my magick from me that I am unable to protect myself."

Reign could hear his smile on the other end of the phone, and she knew he was right. If she wanted to help her father, she had to first help herself. But between Nicola, Donovan and his cohorts, Krystian, the gallery and being Alexa's maid of honor, her plate was full to the brim. Not to mention that if any of her grandparents did decide to pay her a supernatural visit, it was almost guaranteed *not* to be a social call.

"Okay, Okay...so you're right for once," Reign teased. "But just know that I will be checking up on you frequently. I lost Paw Paw, I can't lose you too."

After three years of being rejected by his only child, Julien could almost feel his heart swell with love at her words. Even if someone had taken his life at that very moment, he'd die happy knowing that he was loved by the one person left on earth that mattered to him.

"No worries over me, you've already made me proud mô piti. And soon, all who come for us will fear the light that has manifested in you. It is important to remember the strength of your bloodline, because it is like no other."

Julien's words brought an overflow of both apprehension and excitement to Reign. She'd always been intrigued by the beautiful superheroine types that got the man *and* the eliminated the bad guy. The woman men wanted and other women wanted to be. Although, 'getting the guy' didn't seem like it was in the cards for her at the moment.

"If I could be even a little of who you've been able to become despite everything, I think I'll be fine," Reign replied.

"Princesse, you *are* half me *and* half Claudette La' Roche. All of which makes you an amazingly extraordinary woman. Now, enough sentiment; time to get to work."

Reign's talk with her father was comforting, and gave her the strength she needed to take the necessary next steps. While lighting the light blue and yellow candles, she could not help but to think that her father's part in her current mood had been strategically planned out. Reign knew she had to trust her guides more.

Assuming the lotus position on the floor, she closed her eyes and began to chant. Focusing on the necessary chakra spirits to continue her enlightenment progression, she was overcome by a powerfully calming scent. Feeling more at ease this time around, after only a few minutes Reign opened her eyes and inhaled the pleasant citrus and lavender aroma that filled her nostrils. Upon doing so, what she saw was just as enjoyable a shock as the scent she'd breathed in.

Where she now stood, the ground was covered in a pale yellow and felt amazingly soft under her bare feet. Glancing up, Reign saw open sky and thought it looked marvelously blue, stretching so far that it didn't seem to end. Closing her eyes, she lifted her face to the warming yellow sphere that hung high, marveling at its comfort.

Looking down, Reign saw that she was clad in a flowy tulip yellow satin gown with powder blue stitching that accented her form. This place was drastically different than that of Muladhara, Anja and Sahasrara. And she somehow felt an unseen embrace that comforted her, taking away whatever doubt and worry she may have had.

"My child, so you have finally taken the next step to becoming the truest version of self," a voice said.

Reign looked around, taken aback by how the voice came to her. It wasn't necessarily filling the space she was in; it was more like a hushed tone drifting on the tailcoats of the breeze that blew carelessly through her hair.

"Yes, I have," she replied assuredly.

Before her eyes the yellow sphere that was just caressing her skin with warmth drifted down, like a slowly deflating balloon. When it landed, it took the form of a lithe, graceful and impossibly beautiful woman. Reign was awestruck as she took in the fiery blue mane and incandescent sapphire eyes of the gorgeous creature before her.

"There is much promise within you child, that is why you were chosen so very long ago. Ancient blood during an ancient time foretold of your coming, but in this life you have had a lengthy slumber."

"And what is it that I must learn from you to continue to…*awaken*?" Reign asked, still breathing in the flowery citrus scent that permeated the air.

"We are here to rouse your emotions and strengthen your spiritual oneness."

Reign couldn't help but to smile.

"My emotions are on overdrive and my spiritual self is probably the only thing I'm sure of right now."

"Is that so?" the figure before her asked.

"Yes," Reign answered, not so sure of herself anymore.

"Walk with me," the woman said, turning and heading toward a field of calla lilies. "First, heightened emotions do not mean all is well. This is a moment when you are likely to lose control of self and be open to the adverse if untrained."

Reign was thoughtful about what was just said to her before deciding to reply.

"As much as I want to disagree, what you're saying does makes sense. I've experienced a lot over these last months that I believe has attributed to my *being stuck* right now."

They walked in silence for a moment before Reign continued.

"Can I ask you something?"

"Sylvie."

"Huh?" Reign responded absently.

"You were going to ask my name. And for now, it is Sylvie."

She wasn't quite sure why, but Reign needed to put some sort of a human quality to the supernatural being that now walked by her side. Doing so made current circumstances seem less surreal.

"Ok Sylvie. So how do I, um, regroup?"

Just as Reign said those words she felt herself begin to sink in the cottony softness of the ground underfoot. She panicked when her feet became suctioned, as though trapped in melted marshmallows.

"You must control and redirect your instinctive emotions. Once you do that, fill yourself with the spiritual completion that you already have and grow it. Let the powers that reside in you become instinctive, allowing them to serve their purpose."

Reign's mind was frozen in fear as she attempted to fight her way out of the sticky goo, which only caused her to sink deeper. And after much struggling, her hands also became trapped.

"Sylvie, please help me. I can't get free," she begged, now down to her waist, arms pinned by her side.

The once bright blue sky darkened and rage filled Sylvie's eyes, turning them a deep cobalt as she spoke her next words calmly.

"If you can't, that simply means you are not worthy after all and your death will be imminent."

Now up to her ribcage in the sludgy goo, the pressure of it began to restrict her breathing. And as fearful as she was, Reign knew there would be no help from Sylvie. Closing her eyes, she redirected her thoughts from impending death to the life that had been laid before her. Every emotion in that moment was harnessed, and she didn't know how, but Reign was able to redirect all of that energy to a force she couldn't explain.

When she'd opened her eyes again, Reign was standing next to a smiling Sylvie and no longer fighting for her life.

"H-how did I do that?" She stammered, looking down at her dress.

"Well, *I* cleaned you up," Sylvie answered with a smile. "You're not *that* good. But everything else, that was all you."

"But...how?"

"Your physical being holds many gifts, but so does your spiritual presence," Sylvie began. "When you're able to channel and harness an energy as powerful as human emotions, you can supernaturally will any other gift to exponentially increase in strength."

"So what, I wished my spirit free and it drug my body with it?" Reign asked, almost laughing.

"Actually, that's not a bad explanation of it," Sylvie affirmed thoughtfully.

Then, in the next instant, Reign was perched high in the branches of a nearby blue jacaranda tree.

"Seriously?!" She screamed, squeezing her eyes shut and hanging on for dear life. Other than snakes, heights were her next biggest fear. "Dear God in heaven, *why* would you put me up here?!"

"By conquering your fear, you conquer your emotion and the ability to manipulate and use it. Harness, focus, direct,"

Sylvie instructed. "And if you do this successfully, we won't have to try a third time with the snake pit."

At those words Reign relaxed and took several calming breaths. This time around, her actions were more deliberate and she could feel her subconscious channel her emotional state. When she opened her eyes again, she was no longer perched helplessly in the beautiful blue tree; Reign was back on the ground and relieved, hoping she'd proven herself to Sylvie.

"We can skip the snakes," she said, with a knowing look in her eyes. "You've done very well, and I am proud."

Sylvie looked down at Reign one last time before ascending back into the yellow sphere that hung beautifully in the sky. Reign was so happy with herself and content that she fell confidently back onto the cottony soft ground and plethora of yellow flowers. However, she had not anticipated that instead, she'd land on the plush carpet of her living room floor.

Chapter 3

Reign continued laying on the floor and was completely perplexed. She knew where she was, but for some reason all she could think about were lemons, lavender and blue trees. It took her a moment to focus and clear the fog in her head before she could remember.

"Sylvie," she mumbled aloud followed by a deep sigh.

If Reign had gathered any extra bit of information during this meditation it was: the fun ends when the spirit leaves. She sat up rubbing the back of her head to take the ache away. Looking at the clock Reign also took note that she's been meditating nearly four hours, and now it was nearly ten at night.

Pushing herself up off of the floor, she walked over and flipped on the light switch, but nothing happened. Thinking her living room bulb blew out, she walked over to the kitchen and flipped on that switch. When she remained enveloped in darkness, panic began to creep up on her. She hadn't made an effort to progress her gifts in months and nothing out of the ordinary had happened. It only made sense that someone, or something, would attempt to attack her once she had.

Besides the light from the candles, Reign's two story home was completely consumed in the inky blackness of night. As she made her way cautiously back to the living room, she didn't know whether to be looking out for her great Grandmother's icy purple eyes, or some assailant hiding in the shadows. Reign was comfortable fighting and using her gifts, but by no means had she mastered any of it.

Just as she decided to call her father Reign's phone rang, scaring her half to death.

"Hey Lex," she answered breathlessly after checking the caller ID.

"Hey, is your power out?" Alexa asked.

Breathing a sigh of relief, Reign informed her that it was.

"It all feels way too coincidental though. It must've gone off sometime during my meditation."

"So, you've finally started again I'm assuming," Alexa inquired.

"Yeah, I got a call from my father. Mom came to him about me. As good as it feels to be a part of this amazing prophesy or whatever you want to call it, I'm not sure I want this hanging over my head. It's a lot of pressure."

"I don't know, seems way too important of a thing to be unsure of. Besides, you turned a crumbling manor into a successful art gallery on your own. Now *that's* pressure."

"Yeah Lex, I know how important this is. It's literally life and death, which in itself is part of the problem. And I also can't help but to wonder if Donovan Tolliver is mixed up in all of this because of who I am…or is it all just happenstance."

"I think you're overthinking everything. This is happening to you whether you like it or not. Now, what you do with it, that's totally up to you. But whatever you decide, you need to be sure."

"Lex…" Reign said shakily.

Alexa immediately noticed the change in her friend's tone, "What's wrong?"

Reign couldn't see a thing in the dim lighting, but her senses told her everything. Someone, or something, was watching her. She didn't know from whom or where the gaze came, but she knew whoever it was had not been doing so with good intentions.

"Nothing, nothing. I'm fine. I just got a weird feeling, like I'm being watched again. That sensation hasn't crept up on me in a while, and I didn't miss it."

"Trust your instincts. If you feel like someone is looking at you, someone probably is. I need you to start trusting yourself more," Alexa stated anxiously.

She didn't know how to take any of what was going on with Reign, but Alexa could not think about the possibility of harm coming to her best friend.

"Ok, so I'm going to check things out around the house. If I don't call you back in ten minutes, call the cops," Reign instructed Alexa.

"So, you want me to get off the phone with you while you walk around alone and Sherlock Holmes your house? That is the dumbest thing you've ever said to me, and you've gotten around to saying quite a few dumb things lately."

"Lex, I can't hear and won't be able to focus with you breathing in my ear. All I need is ten minutes."

After about a minute of hesitation, Alexa gave in.

"Ok, ten minutes. And you better call me back!"

Reign hung up the phone before Alexa could change her mind. Grabbing a poker from the fireplace she decided to start in the upstairs dojo. Tiptoeing as quietly as she could, Reign gave her eyes time to adjust to the darkness. She decided not to carry a candle; reluctant to give herself away to whomever, or *whatever*, may have been watching her. She was amazed when, after deciding to attempt harnessing her fear as Sylvie had guided her to do, she was able to lift a small veil of the darkness. Even though her surroundings looked more like she was staring through cheap night vision goggles, it was better than what the pitch blackness offered only a few moments before.

Reign barely took a breath as she inched her way around the perimeter wall, scanning every corner and opening. When she was sure it was all clear, she began making her way back downstairs, which was still bathed in candle glow.

"I know you're watching me," she whispered. "Who are you and what do you want?"

She didn't really expect an answer, but wouldn't have been completely shocked if there had been one. With all the ghosts and supernatural occurrences that she bore witness to in the last months, nothing could have surprised her. Well, at least that's what she thought before hearing a bang at the front door.

Reign let out a little yelp of surprise before exhaling to calm herself.

"Who is it?" she asked, continuing to descend the steps.

"Detective Amoureux, New Orleans Police Department," the voice said from the other side.

"Ugh, Alexa," she muttered under her breath and swung open the door. "I'm fine; it's only been like eight minutes."

"Excuse me?" the gentleman questioned with a puzzled expression.

Reign looked up and directly into aqua blue eyes that nearly took her breath away. This detective looked like he was straight out of one of those romance novels she used to bury her head in. His short, jet black hair and tanned complexion only brought out his piercing eyes more.

Snapping out of her trance Reign continued. "My friend, Alexa, she called you right? Because I told her I'd call back in ten minutes, but it's barely been nine," she realized she was rambling, but couldn't seem to stop herself. "And if you're here already that means she probably called as soon as I hung up."

"Ma'am, no, I'm a detective. I don't answer police calls. I'm here because there was an incident at your neighbors."

Only then did Reign notice the flashing lights of the three cop cars in front of the house next door.

"Oh my…what happened?"

"Were you acquainted with your neighbor at all?"

"Well, yes. I've lived here for nine years. Mrs. Renaud lost her husband a couple years back...." Reign paused in thought. "Wait, you said were. As in past tense? Is she okay?" she asked, a little more panicky than she'd intended to be.

"Mrs..." the detective began.

"It's *Ms.* La'Roche," Reign interjected absently.

"Ms. La'Roche, when was the last time you saw Mrs. Renaud?"

"Two, maybe three days ago," she answered as the very uneasy feeling she'd had grew.

Somehow Reign knew her kindly elderly neighbor was not okay. And what was worse, she was almost sure that *she* was the reason Mrs. Renaud was not okay.

Reign looked up when a tissue appeared before her. She didn't realize she'd started crying, and at the detective's kind gesture the tears began to fall even faster. Reign didn't pull away when he placed his arm on her shoulder in an attempt to soothe her. It was, in fact, comforting. And at that very moment, the power for the entire block was restored. The street and house lights sudden illumination was blinding, causing her to squint just a little.

"This blackout wasn't an accident, was it?" Reign asked, looking up at the detective.

"I can't say for a fact. We're just checking in with the neighbors as a precaution."

Looking at him through tear filled eyes she asked, "Did someone call you? Is that how you knew something had happened to her?"

The detective was very hesitant to continue the conversation, but the agony and desperation in her eyes refuted his better judgment.

"She called. Somehow Mrs. Renaud was able to get to the phone in enough time to dial the police."

"Or maybe whoever did this *let* her get to the phone."

Detective Amoureux was surprised by Reign's assumption, because that had been his suspicion as well. Reaching into his pocket he pulled out a business card, then handed it to her.

"Keep this on you. If you see anything out of the ordinary, no matter the time, don't hesitate to call."

She glanced down at the card he handed her, *Detective Dominic Amoureux, N.O.P.D.* As he stepped back, Reign couldn't help but feel herself drawn to him. There was something in his eyes. Something that pained him greatly, and she was unsure why she was compelled to know what it was.

"This isn't a homicide investigation just yet. We're really just trying to piece things together right now," he lied. He knew the elderly lady had been murdered, but there was no need to add to this woman's already evident pain.

Reign nodded her head in affirmation before asking, "But she *is* gone, isn't she? Mrs. Renaud is gone?"

"Yes, she is. I'm sorry," he answered, then turned and walked away.

Before she could get the door closed, Reign caught the blur that was Alexa racing up her walkway.

"What the hell happened? And why the hell didn't you pick up your phone or call me back? And...what the hell!?"

Reign looked down at her phone and saw the eight missed calls from her friend.

"I thought I told you to call the cops if I didn't call back, not rush over here in a frenzy," she replied, disregarding Alexa's flailing gestures of frustration.

The two walked into the house and Alexa closed the door behind them.

"Well, I knew that I'd get here quicker. Besides, it looks like the entire force is here anyway. Wait, *why* are they here?"

Reign went and sat on the sofa, eyes still red from her emotional breakdown. Alexa walked to the kitchen, poured two glasses of water, then sat by her friend. She sat quiet and patiently while waiting for Reign to gather herself.

"Well, I was doing what I said and checking out the house. When I got back downstairs there was a knock at the door from the detective there," she began, nodding toward the door. "At first, I thought he came because of you. Then he started asking me about Mrs. Renaud."

Her tears began flowing all over again. The elderly woman and her husband had taken to Reign immediately, becoming more like a set of surrogate grandparents to her. They often invited her over to play cards or talk about the latest politics. But what Reign enjoyed most were the weekly Sunday dinners after church. Then when Mr. Renaud passed, Reign made it a habit to visit his wife often, even if only for a short while. Mrs. Renaud still cooked Sunday dinners, but with all the changes in Reign's life as of late, she had missed the last few.

"Is she okay?"

"No, she's dead. And I have this sickening feeling that it's my fault. The way the detective was questioning me, I knew he believed someone had to have hurt her."

"Reign, don't do that. It's no one's fault but the evil asshole that did it. That is *if* a person did it at all. For all you know she could've had a heart attack."

"No, there was too much commotion. And all of those officers and a detective wouldn't have just shown up out of the blue like that for a medical emergency. The entire world knows how much I love you," Reign continued, dismissive of Alexa's attempt at comfort, "what if they come for you too. I'd die if anyone hurt you."

Alexa wrapped her arms around Reign and hugged her tight.

"No one is coming after me. And even if they did, have you seen my fiancé?"

Her words calmed Reign down, but only a little bit and for just a moment. She knew the only way to protect the ones she loved was to keep moving forward with her spiritual and physical progression. She needed to gain control over every power, new and old. Not another person she cared about would come to harm; and anyone that tried would meet a fate far worse than death.

Dominic glanced back at the door as Ms. La'Roche's friend raced past him. She seemed to be in a panic, and in light of current events, that made him very curious as to why. Though he had to admit that when she first opened the door, he was floored. Her skin was a smooth shade of toasted almond, her eyes were as clear as honey and the raven coils that were carelessly piled on top of her head were the perfect backdrop to a masterpiece. And when she'd realized her neighbor had died, instead of caressing her shoulder, what he really wanted to do was cradle her in his arms.

"Detective Amoureux," a nearby cop called out while walking up to Dominic, "did you find anything out?"

"No. Though she took the news pretty hard. I'll get in touch with her again once she's less emotional."

As Dominic walked away from the officer and back into Mrs. Renaud's house, a feeling of grief and anger overtook him when he surveyed the scene. There was blood everywhere and smears on the floor from where the killer had drug her from the door several times as she fought to get free. Who would be sick enough to toy with the old woman, allowing her to continuously try to escape knowing she never would.

He looked at the pictures on the wall, and one in particular caught his attention. It was of Ms. La'Roche smiling while standing in front a huge and dilapidated brick manor. She signed it, *Granny and Pops, I finally did it. Love, Reign.* Dominic looked at the picture intently. He didn't know why, but the house she stood in front of seemed so familiar to him.

The sound of the zipper snapped him out of his reverie. Without turning, he instinctively knew it was the sound of the body bag being closed. He couldn't turn around. He didn't want to see the mutilated face of the sweet old lady that Reign La'Roche affectionately referred to as...Granny.

Chapter 4

It took every bit of strength that Adrian had to keep Krystian from getting out of the house. More than once he'd tried to tackle Adrian down, and failed miserably. Before she left, Alexa had begged him not to get physical; however, Krystian was testing every last bit of his patience.

"Look, I told you she is fine. Alexa is over there right now and there's not a hair missing from Reign's head."

Alexa had used poor judgment by speaking about Reign in front of Krystian. *Especially* since it concerned her safety. And when she called back and told them about the detective and Reign's likely murdered neighbor, Krystian had lost all calm.

"Adrian, I love you like a brother, but if you don't get out of my way…"

"You may as well follow through on your threat, because I *am not* letting you leave. You going over there right now would be the worst idea possible."

"And what exactly could the two of them do if someone broke into Reign's house right now? Is she really ready to take on the brown-nosing sycophants of my psychotic father?" Krystian asked, making another attempt for the front door.

"Krys, there's about a million cops over there. Not to mention Reign just lost somebody else she loved. I doubt she'll take kindly to you trying to alpha male your way into her house. If she is as powerful as you say, but still lacks the ability to control it, what do you think will happen if she sees you?"

Krystian knew he was right, but the need to see no harm had come to her for himself was overwhelming. Seeing Reign at the engagement party had rekindled everything he thought had been at least partly tamed. And *that* was the very reason he'd chosen to stay away from her for so long. To know *of* her whereabouts and doings, as opposed to actually keeping his eyes on her. Reign was like the purest form of absinthe to him. Potent, intoxicating and addictive.

"Look, Alexa is going to stay there tonight. In the morning, we will go over together, I promise you. That'll give you time to get out of your head, because in this place that you're at with Reign right now, the first words out of your mouth can make or break you."

Krystian calmed down and thought about what Adrian just said, and it did make sense. Though there was a part of him that didn't care if Reign never spoke to him again, he just wanted to see that she was safe. But that other part of him crept in and took over. The part that missed the way she looked at him, and how, if he looked at her a certain way, she became flustered. He needed her back in his life.

"Okay, we'll go in the morning."

It was dark and cold. Reign had no idea where she was or how she had even gotten there. The last thing she remembered was falling asleep with Alexa knocked out beside her. The emotions and wine had taken a toll on them both and their bonding session had barely made it past midnight.

"Hello," she called out, "is anybody there?"

The only voice she heard was her own echoing off of the blackness. As Reign began walking, she felt the crunching of gravel underfoot. Feeling the rise of a dooming panic, she remembered how she'd been successful using her harnessed emotions to see in the dark during the blackout, so she tried again. And after a couple attempts, it finally worked.

Looking around, her efforts proved to be futile because she saw nothing but empty space. She took another step forward, but instead of the crunching gravel, she felt a snap under her foot. Looking down, Reign was so shaken by what she caught sight of that not a sound escaped her mouth as she began trembling fiercely. There were tiny bones everywhere. Then, looking back up, the inky blackness had been replaced by walls covered and dripping with blood. And this time, she did scream.

Reign woke up to a cold rag being pressed to her face and Alexa and Adrian staring down at her with concerned expressions.

"What is going on," she asked, sitting up in bed.

"You've been tossing and turning in your sleep for the past hour. I tried to wake you, but you wouldn't so much as crack your eyes open. Then, just about fifteen minutes ago, you started sweating buckets."

Reign looked down at the front of her shirt and, sure enough, it was drenched in sweat. Even the front of her shorts were sticking to her due to how bad she had been perspiring.

"And when did Adrian get here?" she asked with a forced smile and closed her eyes.

Adrian and Alexa exchanged glances.

"Um, Adrian and Krystian got here around eight," Alexa answered, taking a step back from the bed.

Reign's eyes flew open and rested on Adrian, "You *and* Krystian came?"

"Look, it was either that, or have him patrolling the perimeter of your house like it was Fort Knox," he said, placing his hands up in defense. "He heard about your neighbor, then with the blackout. He just wanted to know you were safe."

At those words, Krystian entered the room. He looked tired and disheveled, but even in that state, he was still absolutely gorgeous. Reign didn't know if she wanted to hurl herself at him and kiss him, or see if one of her new powers included shooting lightening from her hands. It was only extremes when it came to Krystian, the in-between didn't exist.

"Hey. Look, I just wanted to see for myself that you were okay. I won't get all militant if you preferred I left," Krystian said.

Looking at him Reign could tell he meant every word, though she knew he would've rather stayed. Truthfully, she was too drained to even put up a fight. So she nodded and closed her eyes again for a moment, allowing the sound of the heavy raindrops beating against the window soothe her.

Alexa and Adrian understood the temporary truce that Reign allowed Krystian, and they were both glad for it. Neither one of them wanted to have to pick sides between the two.

"Ok, so I'm going to jump in the shower really quick. And I guess when I'm done ya'll will probably want to know why I look like I took a bath with my clothes on."

"You sure you're okay?" Alexa asked as Reign began to push herself up off of the bed.

"Yeah, I'm fine. I just need to take a hot shower and clear my head for a second."

When they were sure she was steady, the three companions left Reign in her room alone and closed the door. Once they did, she dropped back down on the bed and began trembling fiercely as the images from the dream flashed in her mind. Then she remembered the stench. It was a putrid mix of sulfur and the poignant metallic smell of blood.

Reign had an idea what the dream meant. Nicola had never left; she was just waiting for an opportunity. *But an opportunity for what?* That's what frightened her; she couldn't figure out Nicola's motives. There was one thing for certain though, Reign needed to find out what had happened to Mrs. Renaud. She needed to know if her attacker had been human…or was it something else.

Once Reign exited the shower, she immediately noticed that her bed had been made and the scent of food wafted under her bedroom door. Her stomach began growling almost instantly.

When she walked out of the room wearing oversized sweatpants and a t-shirt, she saw that Krystian was the one doing the cooking. Adrian and Alexa sat nearby at the island, and the trio were having an intense debate about butter.

"Margarine is *not* butter," Krystian said heatedly. "Butter is for cooking dishes, margarine is for…toast!"

"Look man, butter, margarine, it's all the same. Toast, grits, some fancy French meal…it's still the yellow stuff that makes things delicious," Adrian commented with a chuckle.

"Seriously? The great butter debate is what's been going on for the past thirty-ish minutes?" Reign asked with a straight face. Although it took all of her willpower to not burst with laughter.

Krystian looked up and the second they made eye contact, he turned to flip whatever he had cooking on the stove. Reign joined Alexa and Adrian at the island, then provided a disclaimer to remain neutral regarding the dairy dispute. There was no way she was getting involved with that.

"Well, your timing is impeccable as always," Krystian said, turning and placing a plate in front of her. Then he did the same for Alexa and Adrian.

Reign stared at the heaped plate before her. A cheese omelet, French toast, grits, and a quarter of a turkey sausage.

She was about to take her first bite when she noticed the empty chair next to her, and that Krystian was standing as he ate.

"Really?"

He looked at her questioningly while Reign continued to purposely stare at him. He was seemingly oblivious to what he was doing.

"You *can* sit down you know. I'm not going to lash out at you in some uncontrollable frenzy. And I promise my grits will go from my plate to my mouth."

He gave in and sat down next to Reign, then they ate in companionable silence. All Reign heard was chewing and the clink of forks. The food was just that good.

"Thanks for making my bed. You know you didn't have to do that," Reign said to Alexa.

"Um, I didn't," she replied.

"I did. And I know I didn't have to, but you have enough on your mind without having to worry about linens too. Besides, I wasn't doing anything anyway," Krystian interjected, keeping his eyes on his plate.

"Well, thank you then. I do appreciate it," she responded, feeling slightly awkward.

Nothing else was said until they had finished eating. Alexa washed the dishes, Adrian dried and Reign and Krystian sat on the sofa in uneasy silence. To Reign, there was so much tension between the two of them that they may as well have been sitting a mile apart.

"So," Alexa said, sitting on the loveseat and looking directly at Reign, "let's start with the obvious."

She was quiet for a second, then inhaled deeply. Reign didn't want to go back to that place that held her hostage in sleep, but she knew it was all a part of a process. That and the fact that the three people that sat staring at her had no intention of letting it go that easily.

"I had another dream, but it felt so much more real than they have in the past. It was unnaturally dark, kind of musty, and it felt like I was walking through one of those unpaved parking lots. Then, I could see," she didn't want to share the details of her new abilities just yet. "Suddenly the walls were coated and dripping with blood. The ground was no longer covered in rocks, but tiny bones. And the smell went from putrid to overpowering. I didn't see anyone, but I felt *everything*. It was like all of my senses were on overdrive."

Krystian sat there watching her and saw how she began to tremble. He had no way of actually knowing the fear she felt, but what he saw in her eyes was enough to make him want to reach out and comfort her. But he stopped himself. If he wanted another chance with her, he had to start over.

"Well, there is something else," Alexa began. "You were repeating something over and over. That's when you started sweating."

Reign looked at her in shock, "I said something…aloud?"

"Yeah, though it took me a few times to get it. *Kifo ulikuwa mwanzo*," Alexa said, answering Reigns unasked question. "Do you know what that means?"

"Yes, actually I do. It means, *death was the beginning*," Reign answered. "But I have no idea what language it is. And before any of you ask…no I haven't heard it before, so I have no clue how I even understand it."

"Okay, so this is getting stranger and stranger by the minute," Adrian commented before resting his head in his palms. Then he looked up and confessed, "I have to be honest, I doubted you all's sanity when Krys first told me what was going on. But after being here the last few hours, *I'm* starting to feel like the crazy one."

"Hey Adrian, I know this is a lot to take in, and if you want out I totally get it. I'm sure from here on out it's not going to get any better," Reign said, getting up and sitting on the table in front of him. "You and Lex are about to start a life together, and there's no way I'd expect ya'll to get tangled in my mess."

There was slight hesitation before Adrian spoke, "Nah, you can't get rid of me that easily. I said I *thought* I was crazy, I never said I was prepared to turn my back on one of the most important people to my fiancé and me. You need us, and by default we're obligated to be there for you."

"Well in that case, there's something each of you needs to know," standing up, she walked back over to her seat on the sofa with Krystian. "I'm getting much stronger and I have powers now that were I guess…dormant, before."

"Like what?" Krystian asked. It was the first time he'd spoken since they'd finished eating.

"Well, it's a little hard to explain. But basically, I can channel whatever emotion I'm feeling and use it to amplify something else. For instance, during the blackout I was able to turn on a kind of night vision, which allowed me to see in the dark. Basically, I took all of the fear I felt and, for lack of a better term, wished it to my eyes."

All three of them stared at her as if she had just grown a second head. So Reign got up and closed the heavy blackout curtains on all of the windows. The sky was still overcast and dark, which allowed only gloom to pierce through the loft windows. Now in the nearly pitch black living room, no one said a word. She knew they wanted to believe her, but just needed a little convincing.

Reign did the first thing she could think of. Making her way around the kitchen and dining room with her night vision-esque sight, she specifically grabbed two wine glasses and two snifters without incident. Reign then filled the first two with Alexa's favorite white wine, and into the latter she poured a generous amount of brandy. Then, when she was done, placed each glass in front of the respective person. But before she could say a word, Krystian broke the silence.

"Reign, you don't have to prove anything to us. *You* believe it, and that's really all that matters."

After this statement, she switched on the lights. There was such satisfaction on Reign's face when she saw their expressions that she couldn't help but to smile.

"As you were saying."

All three of them went for their glasses, downing it in just about one gulp.

"Yup, never doubting you again," Adrian said, once he'd finished his glass.

Chapter 5

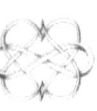After the morning of Reign's nightmare, the next three days had gone by in the blink of an eye. She hadn't dreamt or felt anything since, but refused to get lax.

Now it was Wednesday, the first day of the week for her gallery, and she was thankful for it. Reign was appreciative for something to do other than meditate or get her butt kicked by her relentless Wu Shu instructor, Sato Sensei. He pushed her harder and harder with each training, and at times she felt she was going to snap.

"I'm paying you to train me! What good is it going to do if I get killed in the process?" She screamed during one intense session that had left her hands bruised and swollen.

He then looked at her calmly, and in a way that only he could. "I do not know why you sought me out, but I do know that you are up against a mighty force; I can feel it attacking your chi. My only wish is that you survive it."

Ever since then, Reign pushed through whatever pain and bruises resulted from her frequent trainings. Her mind, body and spirit were weapons in themselves that had to be strengthened and disciplined individually. She had to press on, no matter how painful.

So now, as she entered the doors of The Vieux Carré Vignette, Reign inhaled the rich scent of oak that wafted from the exposed beams of the rafters. There was something so comforting about being there, and in more recent days, had become her retreat.

"Hey Reign," Lisa greeted her from the main reception desk.

It was early, but quite a few guests had already made their way through the Vieux's doors.

"Good morning sunshine. Anything new today?" Reign asked her friend and employee.

"Nothing much, just a couple of private tour requests and an inquiry for a luncheon to be catered off the veranda. You'll probably also have a few voicemails. Some calls came through the minute I turned off the overnight greeting, as if they were just waiting for you."

"Thanks so much Lisa," Reign said, as she started up to her office. "Oh, by the way, do you have plans after work?" She asked, turning back.

"Not if you don't count going home and snuggling with Petey," Lisa replied with a bright smile.

"No, going home to canoodle with your big baby of a dog does not count as 'plans'. Poor dog. I still can't believe you named him *Petey* of all things."

Lisa gave her a, *don't start with me,* look. Reign put up her hands in surrender and continued with her previous statement.

"So I was thinking, how about we go out for drinks. Maybe catch a band and dance 'til our feet hurt."

Dancing was one of Reign's favorite ways to relieve stress. And right now, the anxiety her stress levels were causing was massive. She was so desperate to get out that if Lisa was not going to be a willing participant, Reign planned on going by herself.

"Sounds like a great idea. We haven't been out in a while," Lisa agreed with a relentless smile.

Reign nodded then turned, continuing on to her office.

Three hours into her paperwork and ledgers, Reign's desk phone rang. "Yes?"

"James Alexander is here to see you," Lisa said from the other end.

"You can send him up," she instructed.

Only moments later, there was a knock at the door.

"Come in."

"Well hello there," James said with a smile upon opening the door.

"Well hello to you too. Come in and have a seat," she directed. "I see you're learning to use the proper channels instead of just barging up to my office."

Reign looked at James, unable to understand how she felt nothing other than friendship for the Adonis of a man that was about to take a seat across from her. Tall, well groomed, athletic, clean shaven and chocolate. Reign smiled in appreciation while at the same time wondering what was wrong with her.

She had only known James about three months, but in that time they had become very close. At one point, Reign had almost written him off. His initial persistence was borderline stalker-ish, but in the end, she was glad she decided to give him a chance. James hadn't realized it, but during one of the most difficult times in her life he had become her sanctuary. His kindness was one she vowed never to forget.

"So, what's up Reign drop," he asked, making use of one of the pet names he coined for her.

"Nothing, just inquiries for new business. Oh, that reminds me," she said, getting up and walking over to a cured obsidian armoire, "I got this last week, but I don't think it fits with my office décor at all. Do you know someone that may want it?" Reign asked as she pulled out a large thirty by forty canvas.

"You have got to be kidding me," James said, getting up and walking over to her. "Why, no *how*, did you do this?"

He was in awe and full of emotion while staring at the painting that Reign delicately leaned against the wall. It was of a woman holding her newborn son, and the look in her eyes were full of such love that it nearly jumped off the canvas. The portrait was copied from a worn-out picture of James and his mother that Reign had taken from his house in secret, then painted.

"Reign drop, you shouldn't have."

"Believe me, I could never repay you for your kindness. This is just a token of a portion of my appreciation. Besides, it's the only picture you have of you as a baby with your mom, and the original is on its last leg."

"Okay, we're going out for drinks after you finish here," James ordered with finality, blinking away the tears that had begun to sting his eyes.

"I can't, Lisa and I are already going out," she replied with earnest regret.

"So we all go. Drinks, food, whatever either of you want. It's on me."

James really was too good to be true. She never would have guessed that, under his arrogant and tough exterior, there was this sweetheart of a man. Of course, if she ever confronted him about his sweet and sentimental gooey center, he'd go to his grave denying it.

After leaving work, Lisa rode with Reign to her house and James followed. It didn't make sense having two vehicles out when they were all going to be together. Then, the trio decided to head to a nearby bar just off Canal St. whose walls constantly permeated with the soulful sounds of a local live band.

"Thank you ladies, for allowing me to intrude in on your girls' night," James said once they'd parked and were walking toward the bar.

As they entered Reign noticed that, for a Wednesday, there were a fair amount of people out. And for reasons all her own, that's exactly what she'd needed. She had been faced with so much in such a short amount of time and it had begun to take its toll. Reign craved to be around people that knew nothing about her and expected nothing from her. This was so contradictory from the recluse she was only months prior.

"It's always a pleasure to have a man easy on the eyes tagging along," Lisa replied to James with a smile. "Besides, with you here, that lessens the chance that some knucklehead will get too confident."

James looked at her questioningly.

With a small grin, Lisa answered his unasked question, "To be completely honest when we go out, more often than not, it really is for drinks and the music. Like you said, a girls' night. Now, unfortunately for the opposite sex, their radar picks up on us as looking for *attention*."

"Ahhhh, *attention*," James restated wiggling his eyebrows.

Both Lisa and Reign burst into laughter at his telling gesture.

"Yes," Lisa continued, "so you see, you being here just alleviates all of that extra from jump. Because even if you were say…our cousin, you are by far the only alpha-male in this bar, and no one is going to test you to find out what we are to you."

Heading to the table, Reign could already see that sparks had begun to fly. With the not so subtle flirting on Lisa's part, and the open and honest reciprocation from James, it was just a matter of time. Reign really had rather made her way to the dance floor, but was cut short when James motioned for her to come over.

"I know you want to dance twinkle toes, but there is something that we must do first."

He ordered a round of shots that, once they arrived, were immediately downed. Then he sat at their table sipping on cognac while the ladies headed to the dance floor. James was a very laid back kind of guy. He loved the music and the feel of his surroundings, but preferred to enjoy it from a chair. Besides that, if the ladies planned on going out anyway, he was glad to be there to keep an eye on them.

The bluesy music began filling Reign in an inexplicable way, and she danced until her hair was dripping with sweat. Music had always been a passion of hers, and she loved the feeling the rhythmic tones sent through her body. She was just getting into her second wind when Lisa approached her.

"I wanted to ask you something," she said, leaning into Reign so she could be heard over the music.

"What's up?"

"I was just curious about you and James. Is there anything going on between the two of you?" she asked.

Reign smiled, "No, nothing at all. We're just good friends."

Lisa knew she didn't need to say anything else. Her and Reign had been friends long before The Vieux Carré Vignette had come into existence, and now they were as close as sisters. Reign was aware of Lisa's interest in James and wouldn't stop her from expressing it. She also knew that, at this point in their friendship, she would never see James as anything other than a dear friend and that he was okay with it.

When Lisa squeezed her hand before walking over to sit with him, Reign's heart warmed a little. She somehow knew they would be good for one another. But she also had to wonder...would anyone ever be good for her.

Reign was fully aware that sneaking out of the bar and leaving James and Lisa was probably very poor decision making on her part. But she had been danced out, and her friends where so caught up in each other that she didn't want to bother them. Besides, the sun had only just gone down, so total darkness was still at bay. Then, with one final look back before exiting the bar, Reign began her thirty-minute walk home.

The air was balmy as Reign looked in awe at the full moon hanging in the barely-night sky. She had danced hard and the warm evening did nothing to cool the sweat that still dripped from her skin. Closing her eyes and inhaling deeply, she could smell the seafood and spices from the nearby restaurants. Everything about her city was so calming, and yet exciting.

It was upon crossing Lafitte Avenue that Reign had a feeling that something was wrong. When the hairs on the back of her neck rose, she turned to look behind her, but saw nothing. She hastened her step, knowing it was only another ten-minute brisk walk to her house. But at that moment, even five minutes would have been too long.

It was when she reached St. Ann that whoever had been following her finally made a move. Unfortunately for Reign, she did not react fast enough and the air was knocked out of her lungs as she was tackled to the ground. The weight of the person pinning her down prevented her from taking in enough air to cry out or yell for help.

"Scream and I'll slit your throat from ear to ear," her attacker said. He had the intense stench of too much alcohol on his breath, but he was not intoxicated enough for Reign to fight off. "That would such be a shame to do to that pretty little face."

In an instant he was up, yanking her with him. She could feel the blood dripping from where she'd hit the side of her head from the fall. Now being dragged into an alley, her fear was replaced by terror as, once more, Reign was thrown to the ground with great force. Looking up everything was so blurry, but she could see that the house her assailant dragged her behind was abandoned. This meant there was likely no one who could, or would care to, help her.

"You're such a pretty little thing," he slurred, and she could smell a putrid mixture of vomit and alcohol reeking from his breath.

Laying there on the cold ground, she could hear the knife wielding drunkard unbuckling his pants. *Focus Reign*, she said to herself. Keeping her eyes closed she visualized all of her fear and anger. Her intention was to radiate the entirety that energy from her palms and use it to force him away from her, but the only thing that happened was that her hands became quite warm.

Reign's fear magnified when he leaned down on her, and the putrid stench of his breath filled her face. Once again, she tried to harness her emotions and transfer the energy to her hands, but this time, nothing happened at all. She couldn't understand what was going on, or why her powers seemed to be fizzling out.

Feeling desperate and helpless, she finally did scream. Reign screamed with everything in her and flung her hands, attempting to make contact with his face as many times and in any way that she could. She'd been trained in martial arts, but in this moment when it would've proven most helpful, the only thing she could think to do was swing like a twelve-year-old girl.

"I told you not to scream," he growled right before his fist made contact with her face. "Now it just gets worse for you from here."

Reign's hands were pinned above her head as he straddled her, and her head was spinning from the blow. She felt the sharp blade of his knife open the skin of her palm. Reign couldn't make sense of much after that, because the next thing she knew, he was gone. Actually, it was more like God Himself yanked the drunken fool off of her.

"Ms. La'Roche, are you ok?"

Reign heard the voice clear as day and felt instant relief. They obviously knew who she was, but she was unable to focus her eyes.

"If you can hear me, I'm taking you to the hospital."

"No," Reign mumbled, barely audible. "Please, home. I want to go home."

She felt gentle hands touch hers, then glide over her face. She thought it felt like he was checking her injuries, but she couldn't be sure. The next thing Reign knew, she was lifted in the air and being carried somewhere. She probably should have been scared, but everything inside her told her she was safe.

As she was being carried away Reign slipped into unconsciousness, and so, did not catch the amethyst eyes that pierced through the darkness of the alley where she had just been accosted. The eyes of the one that called for her blood, and would not stop until it was obtained.

Chapter 6

When Reign finally woke, she had no clue where she was. The only thing she could tell was that it was still night and she was lying in a bed, but it wasn't her own. Sitting up, her skull was instantly on fire. Reign quite literally felt like somebody jabbed her in the head with a hot poker. Keeping her head down, she swung her legs over the side of the bed and attempted to stand up.

"Whoa whoa, careful there," came a voice from out of the shadows.

Reign was immediately on the attack, but her injuries left her weak and she fell to the floor.

"Please, please don't hurt me," she said as tears fell from her eyes.

"I'm not going to hurt you Reign. Come on, let's get you back on the bed."

Strong arms scooped her up off of the floor and gently placed her back into the mass of pillowy softness.

"Okay, I'm going to turn the light on now, so cover your eyes," the man said.

Reign did as she was instructed, and when the light came on, she had to give her eyes a minute to adjust. Once they were, she looked up at the man sitting next to her in shock.

"Detective Amoureux? How did I end up here?" She asked, looking around and taking in the cozy décor of the room she'd been resting in.

"You were attacked. I found you just in time, but you were adamant about not going to the hospital. I had to make sure you were okay, so I brought you here. And please, call me Dominic."

"Okay Dominic, and where is here?" Reign asked, looking back at her host through squinting eyes.

By everything good and pure this man was beautiful. His eyes were so alluring that they should have been considered a weapon. His midnight hair was disheveled in that sleepy way, and the look he gave almost caused her to forget to breathe. Reign caught herself staring at the wisps of hair on the back of his neck and wondered how it would feel to play in it.

"This is my home. We're in St. Bernard."

"St. Bernard?"

Reign got up, still lightheaded, and slowly made her way to a nearby window. The room she was in faced the front of the property. Unable to see much in the dark evening sky, she was only able to make out the vastness of the land that the house sat on. When she turned back, Reign was taken in by the beauty and architecture that surrounded her.

Now that her eyes had finally adjusted, she was able to see that the room was bathed in shades of blue and gold. The entire space around the room remained decisively masculine. But there were also subtle touches, like the embroidered chaise lounge and sheer navy canopy with its gold etchings, which gave the room a touch of femininity.

Reign's eyes went back to the chaise, because she noticed the blanket and pillow that were on it. Then she looked at Dominic, who had remained patiently seated on the bed as she'd taken in her surroundings. His tanned skin and weathered hands gave the impression of a laborer, not a New Orleans detective. He was staring at her so intently, but did not utter a word.

"Thank you," Reign said finally, breaking the silence.

"You don't have to thank me. Honestly, I just wish I had gotten there sooner," he replied, standing up and walking over to where she stood. "And I didn't want to leave you to wake up in a strange place alone, so I just stayed there," Dominic added, making reference to the slept-on chaise.

Reign started to take a quick step back, then stopped herself. He wasn't going to hurt her. If there was one thing she was certain of, it was that no harm would come to her at the hands of Dominic Amoureux. Of course, she'd thought the same thing about Krystian and look where that had gotten her.

"I'm sorry. I didn't mean to startle you, I just wanted to check your bandage," he said, taking a step back.

"Bandage?" Reign repeated, then touched her forehead. Her hands ran across the oversized gauze pad that was taped there, and that's when she noticed her hand was wrapped too. "Do you have a mirror?"

"Yeah, over here," Dominic answered, getting up and walking her to the adjoined bathroom. She was still a little unsteady on her feet and he wanted to be there in case she missed a step.

It wasn't until he was standing next to her that Reign realized Dominic wasn't wearing a shirt. He was bare chested, wearing flannel pajama bottoms and his eyelids were still quite heavy with sleep. Everything about him was unsettling, and it irritated her that someone she barely knew could have such an effect on her...*again*.

"I got it, thanks," she said, without looking up once they'd reached the bathroom door.

Bracing herself using the wall, she slowly inched her way to the double vanity mirror. Keeping her head down for a moment, she prepared herself for the worst. When Reign looked up, she knew that no amount of preparation could have readied her for the face that she now saw staring back.

The gauze on her forehead hid an obvious gash, but she could still see where the blood had begun to seep through. Her opposite eye was red, black and blue and swollen, and there was a cut above her lip just as bruised and discolored. Reign used her hand that wasn't wrapped to peel off the band-aid on her temple that hid a light scrape while fighting back tears.

"It looks a lot worse than it really is. You'll be better in no time," Dominic said when he noticed her eyes welling up.

"Yeah, I know. It's just that…I thought I was strong enough to protect myself. How can I protect those I love if I can't even protect myself?"

Dominic immediately thought she was referring to her neighbor, Mrs. Renaud. He didn't know what to say or how to comfort her, so he stepped into the bathroom and rested his hand on her shoulder. They stood there in silence for a moment before Reign inhaled deeply, then she looked up at him through his reflection in the mirror.

"I'm guessing a forty-minute ride back to the French Quarter isn't going to happen tonight, so I won't keep you up anymore," Reign said with only mild sarcasm.

"No, it's not," Dominic answered matter of factly. "Besides, you need to get some rest."

Turning to walk back into the bedroom, she stood looking up at him for a moment. "Why didn't you take me to the hospital? I mean, I know you said I was adamant about not going, but why did you listen?"

"I'm guessing you had your reasons. Your wounds were superficial and thankfully nothing more happened than you getting banged up a bit. You'd already been through so much pain and disappointment; I didn't want to be another reason for you to be left hurting or upset."

Reign gave a partial smile before nodding and sidestepping around him. She kept her head down as to avoid another headache she was sure any direct light or abrupt movement would cause. That's when she saw what she was wearing.

"The missing shirt," she mumbled to herself, and suddenly her precarious situation she found herself in felt all too intimate.

"Did you say something?" Dominic asked as she climbed back into the huge four poster canopy bed.

"Oh, I was just saying that I wasn't feeling too alert. You're right, I do need some rest."

Reign pulled the covers over herself and buried deep down into to the bed. There was no reason she should've felt safe being alone with a man she'd met only once, let alone be okay with sleeping in his nightshirt. But she was. First Krystian now Dominic. Where she'd pushed just about every man away that tried to enter her life *for* her entire life, what was it about these two that tugged at her. And as Reign closed her eyes and began to drift off, she missed the look that Dominic gave her before turning out the light. A look that said, he was wondering the same exact thing about her.

It was around eight in the morning when Reign woke up to the sound of rain beating down on the window. She felt mentally well rested as she slowly climbed out of the king-sized bed and limped to the window. It was dark and gloomy, but even with that she could tell that she underestimated the expanse of Dominic's estate. This had to be a family heir property, because there was no other way to explain how a detective could afford it.

Standing there, Reign was suddenly hit with all levels of pain at once. Her face felt like it had been beaten with a mallet, and nearly every part of her body was sore. She needed something for the pain, and when she turned to walk back to the bed, Reign saw her saving grace. Dominic had left two ibuprofen tablets and a bottle of water on the night stand, which she took without hesitation.

After waiting for the pills to take effect, Reign wanted to go downstairs and find Dominic, but she was missing pants. She didn't want to be intrusive, but she didn't want to walk around three quarters naked either. So, after peaking in the closet, Reign was relieved when she came across some sweat pants. Of course, they were much bigger than her normal big, but she slid them on anyway.

Leaving the room, Reign headed down a nearby staircase. While making her descent, she looked at the paintings and plaques that draped the walls all around her. There were men and women dressed in clothing that had to have dated back to the early eighteen-hundred's. And when she reached the landing, Reign came face to face with a portrait just as dated as the rest, but chillingly resembled Dominic Amoureux.

She was openly gaping at the painting when a movement from outside was caught in her peripheral. It was Dominic, this time with his shirt on, coming from a nearby barn and sloshing through the muddy lake that was quickly becoming his front lawn.

"Hey, I see you finally made it out of bed," he said, grabbing the waiting towel from off a nearby hook and tousling his hair dry.

She usually wasn't one to gape, but that's exactly what Reign was doing as Dominic stood there, completely drenched. His navy button up clung to him like a second skin, showing off his well-formed body. And his jeans were so sopping wet they must've weighed a ton.

Unbeknownst to Reign, as she stood there wordlessly admiring him, Dominic was doing the same to her. She was still in his nightshirt, which was entirely too long, and found a pair of his sweat pants that were hanging on for dear life. Then with one look at her bruised face he was reminded of why he attempted physical labor in the torrential downpour that was taking place outside.

When Dominic woke around six that morning he went to check on Reign, who had still been sleeping like a baby. He looked at her face and bandaged hand that was resting on the pillow and was immediately filled with rage. *How* could someone do that? As if she hadn't been dealing with enough already. That's when he decided he needed to go outside and cool off. Dominic was feeling oddly protective of her and he was unsure as to why.

"Are you hungry?" He asked, taking off his boots and leaving them outside.

"Actually yeah, I am," Reign replied, realizing that she hadn't even been conscious of how hungry she was.

Running up the stairs, Dominic called out, "Feel free to look around while I change. Grace, would you mind throwing something together for breakfast." He didn't even wait for a reply as he disappeared into one of the rooms.

"Right away sir," came a voice from a room to the left of the staircase.

Reign wanted to explore the house, but she was also curious about who it was that was now cooking her breakfast.

Looking out the window she frowned in realization that they would not be headed to take her home anytime soon. However, this would likely give her plenty of time to explore the house though. So, Reign decided to give in to her nosiness and seek out the voice named Grace.

Heading to the left, Reign admired the décor. The house had all the feel and magnificence of its nineteenth century splendor, but was also undeniably modern.

Entering the parlor with all of its paintings that showed off a very prominent family, she was impressed by its lavish simplicity. There was even a harpsichord displayed proudly off the center of the room.

Reign was brought out of her wonderment when she heard a sizzle, which was soon after followed by a glorious smell. Her growling stomach made it impossible to stay focused on her surroundings, so she decided to find the source of the sizzle and aroma.

When she walked through the kitchen doors, Reign did not doubt that she'd just stepped foot into every chef's dream. There was a stove larger than anything she'd seen in real life, pots and pans were sparkling and hanging from ceiling mounts, and baskets of bread, fruits and vegetables sat on a huge table in the middle of the room. She quite literally felt like she'd taken a step back in time.

"Bonjour mademoiselle. Following your nose I see," a kindly lady said as she chopped away at the pile of onions in front of her.

Reign smiled at the observation. "Yes, you definitely got me there. It smells amazing. What are you making?"

"Oatcakes, scrambled eggs, a bit of hasty pudding, corn and ham fritters and sliced strawberries. Some good hearty food to take the dampness from your bones."

Reign instantly liked Grace. She must've been around seventy and sported a heavy French accent. She was a stout woman, but her chubby hands were chopping and mincing with the certainty of the most proficient chef.

"Viens ici chérie," Grace said, waving Reign over to her. "Oh no, what happened to you?"

To most other people, Reign would have probably told them to mind their business; but the concern of the busied woman in front of her was a comfort she rather enjoyed.

"I was attacked last night on my way home."

Grace let out a quick gasp, "Oh chérie, who could do this to such a lovely face?"

"I wish I knew," Reign replied, beginning to get angry at the helplessness she had been subjected to. "But thankfully Dominic was there, and most likely saved my life."

Reign's mouth began watering when Grace pulled the oatcakes from the oven and piled them on a platter in front of her.

"Go on, take one," Grace said with a smile. "My Nicky is a good good man. I don't know what I would do without him."

Reign smiled at her and was happily chomping on an oatcake when Dominic walked in, freshly showered and wearing black jeans and a black t-shirt. If she hadn't known any better, she'd say his look was almost menacing.

"Gracie my love, are you boring our guest?" he asked, stealing an oatcake from the tray.

"Si vous continuez à m'insulter, je vous ferai cuisiner votre propre petit déjeuner," Grace replied in what sounded like a threat.

Reign looked up at Dominic questioningly. Her French was good, but not *that* good.

"She's threatening me with kitchen labor. I think we should leave now, because if we have to eat my cooking, we will all die of either starvation or food poisoning," he said with a very sneaky smile. "Besides, I want to take a look at your hand and forehead."

Reign was once again jarred back to the reason she was now trapped in what was quickly becoming a paradise island since the rain hadn't let up.

Dominic had walked her to a room in the house she had yet to see. This was probably the most modern room in the huge plantation era home. There was a sixty-five-inch flat screen television hanging on the wall, and the sofa and loveseat set was plush and very comfortable. Just like much of the house, this room was very masculine, save the burgundy hand stitched curtains and gold leaf décor. And Reign could have sworn that in the onyx backsplash of the fireplace were tiny ruby-like stones.

"Ok, hold your head up," he instructed, sitting next to her. "I'm going to be as gentle as I can."

Reign tried not to flinch as he pulled the gauze from her forehead. She felt like someone was trying to rip her skull open and could not control it when her eyes began to water.

"Well, I know it probably hurts like hell, but it actually doesn't look that bad. I think we should keep the bandage off."

Then, he reached for her hand. The way he gently cupped it as he began unwrapping the gauze was almost intimate, and she couldn't bring herself to look him in the eyes.

Dominic sighed, "Luckily the idiot just grazed your hand. It probably looked worse than it was at the time because it wouldn't stop bleeding. I think you just may live Mademoiselle La'Roche."

For in instant their eyes locked and Reign couldn't tear herself away from those impossibly blue irises.

"Come my dears, it is time to eat," Grace called, peaking her head into the room.

When Reign entered the dining room with Dominic, she was in awe at the amount of food that covered the table. And after she sat down, Dominic called for Grace, someone named Phillipe and Gerald.

Once they were all seated, Grace explained, "Phillipe is my husband. We have both been working for the Amoureux's for as long as we can remember."

"Bonjour," Phillipe greeted her with a warm smile and nod upon entering the dining room.

"And this is Gerald," Grace said of the slim grey-haired man that entered soon after. "He tends to the stables and is the only person Nicky will trust with his horses."

"Nice meeting you Miss," the kindly man responded with a nod.

"Hello, it's very nice to meet you both," Reign replied, returning a smile.

The group talked and ate plenty. Reign hadn't known a time when she'd enjoyed such rich food. Everything tasted so fresh and exploded with flavor. And as they moved from subject to subject and the house filled with laughter, Reign was able to momentarily forget all of her worries and troubles. She was able to forget about the tears, heartache, heartbreak and threat of death that constantly loomed over her... only twenty miles away.

Chapter 7

The rain was relentless all day in the St. Bernard Parish and the wind was fierce. But Dominic was an attentive host as he escorted Reign around the Amoureux plantation house. Then he promised that after dinner he would take her to see the wine cellar, which dated back to the early eighteen hundreds. It was the only part of the house that had been exempt from renovations, undergoing only a couple of minor repairs over the years.

Reign was so engrossed in learning about Dominic's family and the plantation that she had forgotten all about her friends. Then out of the blue a call on his cell phone snapped her back to reality. She waited until he got off of the phone before inquiring about her missing cell phone.

"Did you happen to see it or pick it up?" She asked, referencing the night that he saved her from the drunken rapist.

"No, actually I didn't. But to be fair, I wasn't looking for it either. If there is someone you need to call, you are more than welcome to use my phone."

The truth was, Alexa's was the only number Reign had memorized. Though in all honesty, she really only wanted to talk to her father. He needed to know that she was okay and she'd deal with the rest when she got back.

"Yeah, can I please? My family is probably worried sick about me, and I haven't thought to call anyone until just now."

Taking the phone he handed her, Reign sat on the stairs once they'd descended and dialed Alexa's number.

"I'm just going to give you a little privacy and go check on dinner. You can join us in the kitchen when you're done," Dominic said, then exited the foyer.

On the third ring, Alexa picked up.

"Hello."

"Hey Lex, it's me."

"Oh my...where have you been?! We've been looking everywhere for you! Calling and calling. Then when Lisa told me you were with her last, we tried to retrace your steps and found your phone. *Why* would you walk home and *where* are you!?"

Reign waited for Alexa to take a breath and calm down before she started talking.

"First, I'm fine. I know it was stupid of me to walk home by myself, but I'm ok."

But before she could continue, Alexa cut her off, "Yes, you're okay. I can hear that. What I want to know is where you are?"

"Lex look, I will answer all of your questions happily. But if you cut me off one more time I am hanging up this phone, turning it off and I will see you when I get back home."

"Fine," Alexa replied. But Reign could tell that there was still quite a bit of agitation in her tone.

"First things first. I'm in St. Bernard. The night that I was out with James and Lisa, for reasons all my own, I decided to walk home. Halfway there I was attacked by some drunken idiot. I got banged up quite a bit, but Detective Amoureux was there and basically saved my life."

"Who's Detective Amoureux?"

"The night that Mrs. Renaud died," Reign couldn't bring herself to say murdered aloud just yet, "he's the one that came to the house."

"Oh. Well as worried for you as I was, I probably wouldn't have remembered even if I had held an all-out conversation with him."

"Ok, well he was going to take me to the hospital but I was adamant about not going. Next thing I know I'm waking up in his house with a bandaged hand and gauze on my head," Reign paused to take a breath and collect herself after reliving that horrible moment.

"I had no idea. I'm so sorry I lost it. I was just concerned, but I'm relieved you're okay. Anyway, why haven't you come home yet?" Alexa asked.

Reign smiled into the phone before answering her, "Well, all day it's been raining like Noah's flood. His front yard looks like it's merged with Lake Borgne there's so much water, but it has slowed up since this morning for sure."

"Well, we haven't gotten a whiff of rain up this way. Just stay safe and hurry home," Alexa said.

"I'm hoping that it dries up enough that we can leave tomorrow; but honestly, this ended up being the unplanned getaway I didn't know I desperately needed."

"Well, as long as you're safe, that's all I care about right now," Alexa replied. "And I'll go ahead and call your dad and let him know you're okay."

"Thanks Lex, you're the best. I'll call you when I get back."

When Reign hung up the phone, she felt like an entire weight had been lifted from her chest. Now that everyone would know she was safe, she could enjoy what was likely her last day there.

Standing up, Reign headed toward the kitchen and smiled at the sounds of laughter that emanated from it. Dominic said that Grace insisted on throwing together a huge dinner. And if huge was anything close to how breakfast turned out, she'd be full for days.

After a few minutes of what felt like family time in the kitchen, Reign excused herself. Ever since Dominic had shown her the bathroom that morning, all she kept thinking about was the oversized free standing tub secluded in its corner. She had two excellent reasons to take advantage of a long bath. First, the ibuprofen was wearing off and her muscles had become increasingly sore. And second, Reign hadn't bathed since the day before, and that alone was reason to want to immerse for an hour minimum.

Anxious to begin her languid soaking, Reign hadn't noticed that a chenille robe had been placed on the bed until after she started running the bath water. And hanging on the back of the closet door was a pair of women's jeans and a cozy t-shirt. Reign smiled when she realized everything was just her size. *When had he gotten the opportunity to get me anything,* she'd thought to herself.

Upon reentering the bathroom Reign immediately disrobed, climbed into the tub and sank down to her neck in bubbles. The steaming water soothed away every ache and pain, and even her worries of the last few days. In fact, she became so relaxed that she drifted off into a deep, and much needed, sleep.

When she woke, Reign was surprised that the water was still quite warm. "I have got to get myself one of these tubs," she said aloud, lathering her body with the sage scented soap. Then there was a knock at the bedroom door, which caused her to jump.

"You okay in there," came Dominic's muffled voice from the other end. "Dinner will be served in ten."

"Yeah, I fine," Reign called back with a smile. "I'll be down in a few minutes."

At the thought of another immaculate meal prepared by Grace's magical hands, Reign quickly finished her bath, dried off, dressed and headed downstairs.

When she entered the sitting room where Dominic was reading, his long legs stretched across the couch, he looked up and smiled.

"I see the clothes fit nicely."

"When did you have time to go to the store? It's been raining cats and dogs all day."

"The night of my heroic rescue," he answered simply. And when Reign looked at him in question, he continued, "I didn't think you'd want to be wearing the same clothes you were just attacked in. And this morning you looked so comfy in my sweats, I didn't want to rain on your parade." Dominic said the latter as he swung his long legs off the couch.

"Well thank you. You've done so much, I doubt I'd ever be able to repay you. Life really has no dollar value."

Reign was still standing in the doorway as she spoke. She couldn't figure out what it was about him that was drawing her in. He wasn't like Krystian, but they both had this brooding masculinity that was so appealing. Then she thought about her entire life, alone and never truly feeling connected with anyone of the opposite sex. Now she meets two men she just can't seem to shake in a matter of months. God had to have a riotous sense of humor to think this one up.

"All I ask is that you join me for a nice dinner with my family," Dominic replied, finally standing up and walking toward her.

"Well, that I can definitely do," she agreed, locking her arm around his and allowing him to lead the way.

When they entered the dining room, Grace had just completed setting the table and was standing next to her chair with Phillipe right beside her and Gerald across from them. Dominic walked to the chair to the right of the head of the table and pulled it out.

"Thank you," Reign said. As she sat, so did Grace, Phillipe, and Gerald, with Dominic taking the head seat next to her.

Reign was overwhelmed by the types and amount of food on display in front of her. There was chicken pie, vegetable soup, grilled salmon fillet, corn bread, lamb chops, roasted potatoes, broccoli and string beans. She couldn't imagine ten people eating that much food, let alone the five of them.

"So, you'll likely be leaving us tomorrow?" Grace inquired with a hint of sadness in her tone.

Reign was caught off guard as she ate a spoonful of the chicken pie. Then looking at Grace, she marveled at the explosion of flavor in her mouth. She'd never had a chicken pie, let alone anything like she was eating at that moment.

"I don't know," Reign answered, looking back at Grace, "if everything tastes as good as this pie, I may never leave."

Phillipe gave a great burst of laughter and Dominic couldn't hide the smile that came across his face if he wanted to.

"Unfortunately, I have to go back to work tomorrow. And I'm sure Reign's family and friends are worried sick over her."

She knew he was right, but being there also felt right. Reign felt like she belonged in that house and could not rightly explain why. So instead of continuing with the somewhat sad talk of her leaving, she grabbed a generous slice of cornbread and stayed in her happy place. Maybe they would finish all of the food after all.

She had never eaten so much in her life. So, when Grace brought out the homemade caramel apple pie and vanilla bean ice cream, Reign wanted to cry. It was part from joy and part from the realization that she may have very well been unable to take another bite of anything. However, not knowing when she'd get the chance again, she accepted the slice. It turned out to be the best decision of her life, right next to starting her own gallery.

"I feel like I stepped back in time being here," Reign said with a smile. She was so focused on eating every bit of the dessert that she missed the glances passed between her companions.

"Well, we are set out of the way from a lot. There's not as much pressure from life if we can get away from *modern* society," Dominic replied before taking a long drink from his pilsner.

"Yeah, I get why you like it. But to have to go back to city life every day, and being a detective at that. You have to be getting thrown in the middle of some pretty horrible things."

Reign's comment took his thoughts to Mrs. Renaud, followed by the memory of her screams and bruised face. He did hate the things he frequently came across. Innocence was often the target of some waste of oxygen. And even though not everyone could be as lucky as Reign, he was determined to at least give them justice in death.

"Nicky, are you ok?" Grace asked, standing up and beginning to clear the table.

"Yeah, I'm fine. Just mentally readying myself for tomorrow. It's going to be a long day."

When Reign stood and started helping Grace, she was shooed away.

"You are a guest in this house and I will not have you touch a thing. You should be enjoying your last evening here, not helping an old lady clean."

Before Reign could fix her lips to protest, Dominic stood and nudged her out of the dining room. "Trust me, you don't want to challenge her on this. It won't end well for you."

He was talking so near to her ear that it felt almost intimate. He was too close for her comfort, and she absently followed his directives without a second thought.

Chapter 8

"So, how would you like to end your night Ms. La'Roche? A good movie, a tenacious game of chess, or imbibe while discussing politics?"

Dominic had lead her back into the room where she'd found him earlier. It was a very cozy space, and sitting there with him so close was a tad bit unnerving as she thought about the options he presented. A movie was too intimate, chess was too intense, and she did not want to participate in anything with him that involved her inhibitions being lowered by alcohol.

The trickling rain on the window broke up the soothing silence in the house and reminded her of seeing him sloshing through the rain that morning. Everything about Dominic fit with the house, and it intrigued her. And just like the house, his presence was undeniable; but there was that much more that was left unseen.

"Honestly, I was actually curious about this house," she answered, hoping he didn't see through her. "Everywhere I look I see a story and so much history that it feels like it must go back centuries. With all of these paintings on the walls and dated furnishings, my imagination ran away with me a bit. This feels like something that would have been passed down for generations," Reign continued, then stared at him intently.

Dominic smiled and thought about how the lovely woman before him was the most amazing creature he'd ever laid eyes on. Her exterior was strong, brave and adventurous; but on the inside, she was loving and gentle…and he could see a small glimpse of it. As Reign sat there staring at him, Dominic sensed she knew she was right, but was on the edge of her seat waiting for him to confirm it.

"Maybe you should've been a detective," he began, then followed with a dramatic pause. "This is inherited land and the house was actually built by my family from the ground up. I come from a long line of Louisianan aristocracy, money and *very* strong will. The latter of which eventually caused a great deal of trouble for my family."

Reign could tell she was about to hear a story and was ready for it. When she curled up on her end of the couch, Dominic got up and went to the closet in the far corner of the room. He pulled out a pillow and oversized chenille throw and gave them to her.

"I fall asleep in this room often. Grace started keeping a blanket and pillow down here after the third time it happened."

And as if on cue, Grace entered the sitting area with two mugs of a steaming peach cider totty.

"I thought this would do you two some good."

Reign smiled as she took the mug, "Thank you. You really are wonderful and I appreciate you so much for making me feel welcome."

After handing Dominic his mug, Grace walked back over to Reign and cupped her face. "Child, you are more than welcome. They'll never come a time when I wouldn't be thrilled to see your lovely face."

Reign watched Grace as she retreated from the room, then gave her full attention back to Dominic. "Okay, I'm ready."

He sipped his drink and looked like he was in deep thought for a moment. Then he looked up and gave her a slight grin before beginning.

"This house was completed in 1742 by my great-great-great-great grandfather, Silas Amoureux. He started building probably around 1740 and he and his brother Antonio constructed the majority of the framework themselves. Silas insisted that only family become familiar with the floor plan, which is the main reason it took so long to construct. People thought he was crazy for refusing outside help, because all through its construction my family was forced to live like paupers on the land.

"Anyway, as I'm sure you know, during this time it was dangerous for people of African descent in the south. Silas was aware of this too. He hated it and desperately wanted to do something about it, but his options were limited. That's when he had the idea to construct this house. Its design was not meant solely for his family, but also with the intention of taking in and sheltering would-be slaves and those on the run. Eventually, this land became known as The Eden Plantation.

"The entire top half of the house was built just like any other of that time, but everything below the line of land was used to house runaway slaves or slaves he had purchased. It was like a community bunker down there, and that's what took up the majority of the construction time to complete. Eventually Silas also came up with the brilliant idea to allow the boarders work the land, but he paid them. This way, he was actually able to keep the façade of being a slave owner so his doings raised no suspicion."

"So, there were no cabins on the land? They all lived *under* the house?" Reign interjected.

"Actually, six cabins were built on the plantation's land, but they were mainly for the slaves he purchased. It was too risky an arrangement for runaways though, who also had labor further out in the field to minimize the chances of being spotted by visitors. To get caught doing something of this magnitude would have had horrific consequences for everyone involved.

"Granpa Silas tried to think of everything to make the arrangements as liberated as possible. So, every week he gathered a group of the occupants and would take them to the market so they could shop. This was to make things seem as though they were selecting goods for him. My family was able to do this for over a hundred years without a hint of skepticism, continuing even after slavery ended.

"In eighteen eighty-nine when my great-great grandfather Dominic Silas Amoureux was born, something changed. Even though slavery had ended by that time, it was still a dangerous period for black people. It was also dangerous for the white people who protected black Americans. Now my great-great grandfather, who is also my namesake, fell in love with one of the boarders. From the moment she walked through Eden's doors, Granpa was taken by Justine Baptiste. He tried without end to reject his love for her, but all of his attempts were futile.

"However, there was something about his new love that he didn't know until it was much too late. She was descended from what Africans called, *Enlightened Ones*. Their existence wasn't widely known, except among those that practiced witchcraft. Witches were a plague to the Enlightened Ones, and they hunted and syphoned their natural born powers of premonition and clairvoyant sight. Tracking gifted people like Justine took a lot of time, and stealing their powers always ended in death. Since the enlightenment could only be manifested by an African descended bloodline, no questions ever arose when one was murdered."

"So, you believe in all of this? Witchcraft, magic and so on?" Reign interrupted.

"I feel like I'd be a fool to deny anything was possible. Granpa documented everything and was so precise. No one that ever knew him would have described him as anything outrageous or questionable."

"I was just curious. Please continue," Reign said, clear that now she had one more reason to like Dominic.

"One day Granpa left Eden for the day to tend to some city business. What he hadn't known though was that a coven of witches had tracked Justine down and had been watching the plantation for days. So when he returned that night, you could imagine his surprise at finding her gagged and tied to a chair in the private dining room. And in his haste to get to his beloved, he was hit on the head and knocked unconscious.

"Maybe twenty minutes or so had passed before he came to, finding himself tied to the chair. His eyes scanned the room for Justine, and when he spotted her, his heart nearly stopped. She was lying on the floor, encircled by candles and in a pool of her own blood. She hadn't died yet, but he could tell that it was rapidly approaching. Five women stood around her chanting, and as Granpa looked at her with tears in his eyes, he was unable to speak.

"From there, everything happened kind of fast. With her last bit of strength, Justine turned her head and looked him in the eyes. In that moment, he said he could feel every ounce of love she had for him. She whispered something inaudibly, and the next moment this blinding light passed from her and entered him. Granpa didn't know what happened, but those witches were so furious he was sure they were going to kill him. But at that moment it didn't matter, because Justine was dead."

Dominic had drifted off as he told the story, but when he focused back on Reign, he saw the tears that welled in her eyes. The moment Justine died had forever changed the dynamics of the Amoureux family, and it's a story that he'd never revealed to anyone before. So why had he been more than willing to share it with this woman who was now watching him from the opposite end of the couch with weepy eyes?

"Wow," Reign said softly, then wiped her tears. "Did he ever fall in love again?"

"He married to keep the family name going, but never loved like that again. From what I understand, once his wife produced a male heir, he never touched her again."

At Reign's shocked expression Dominic felt the need to clarify. "He continued to provide for and keep his family quite comfortable, but if he couldn't make love to Justine, he couldn't make love at all. Granpa wasn't cruel, but he did secret that part of himself away that was only meant for his Jussie."

"Jussie?"

Dominic paled a little at revealing Justine's pet name to Reign. He decided to end the conversation before he said too much.

"It was Granpa's name for Justine. How about I take you on a tour of the cellar? It doesn't look exactly as it did when it was lived in, but is still an amazing sight."

Reign was so excited that she paid no mind to Dominic's seemingly innocent change of subject. "I'd love that," she said with a big smile.

Dominic got up and motioned for her to follow him. Reign wanted to explore the house more, but had been unable to. Now, having her own personal tour, she reveled in excitement while following Dominic past the grand staircase and down a long hallway with varying rooms on either side. She was compelled to peek into each room and marvel at the ornate and vintage décor.

"It's like each room was more beautiful than the last," Reign said after looking into the final one. "I've always been into a more modern look, but your home is breathtaking!"

"Well, I'm glad you approve," he replied, turning a corner and continuing on into a huge library that was covered in wall to wall books. Once they'd entered through the double doors, he stopped and waited for Reign to take everything in.

"This is unbelievable. I've only ever seen floor to ceiling books at a library. There is a lifetime of knowledge in this one room."

"Silas had it built after his son was born. He called it the Gen-Isis Library."

Reign looked like she was in deep thought over the room's name, then burst into laughter when she finally got the connection.

"You know, that's actually pretty good. I like it."

Then Dominic walked over to a corner of the room where a door had been inconspicuously tucked away.

"There was a reason for everything Silas did. The original design of the library was absent of windows, and there were two reasons for that. One, his houseguests would have to pass through here to get to their underground quarters. Secondly, he placed the entrance in this room because he encouraged them to read, or learn to read. Walking through a library every day was a constant reminder that they were respected and seen as equals in his eyes."

"Your great-great-great, is that enough?" Reign asked looking at him very seriously.

"One more."

"Great Grandfather was an amazing man. I think he's someone I would've been honored to meet."

Family history meant everything to Dominic, and as he guided her down the stairway, his respect for her grew. "I think he would've been honored to meet you as well."

They had descended about fifteen steps before finally reaching the bottom, and the only light was from what streamed through the door that remained open upstairs. Then Dominick reached up and pulled a string. When the light clicked on, what Reign saw had her smiling from ear to ear.

"The entrance was converted into a wine cellar around nineteen twenty-five. Turns out this is the perfect environment for housing and aging wine. There are actually quite a few bottles here that date back to the turn of the century."

Reign walked around the room and caressed the bottles like she would a new born baby. "This is amazing. Not saying I'm a wine-o or anything, but this is history. Years of bottling and fermenting process changes."

Dominic reached above her and pulled out a dust covered bottle and handed it to her. Reign took it gently and wiped it off to see the date. "Nineteen-twelve."

"Hang on to that. We'll open it tonight and drink it with the hors d'oeuvres Grace made when she realized you were here. Of course, at the time she wasn't aware this was not a social call," Dominic said, gently tracing the cut that still shown on her forehead.

"Okay," was all she said. For a wine of this quality, Reign was more than willing to renege on her vow to not drink with him.

He smiled at her simple acceptance and continued down a stone hallway. Once they reached the end, another light was switched on. What Reign saw before her this time left her speechless. There was one huge room, and in the center was a long wooden table with maybe fifteen to twenty chairs surrounding it. On one wall was a nice sized wood burning stove, and directly across from the dining table was an oversized fireplace. Then there were twelve doors evenly spaced around the expanse of the wall. Dominic walked to one of the doors and opened it.

"Come take a look," he said once he'd realized that she was too awestruck to move.

Reign walked over to him and peeked in the room. There were two beds, a small fireplace, a desk and chair, a dresser and oil lamp.

"All of the rooms were designed like this. Being underground, it stayed very cool in the summer. As a matter of fact, my family often joined their boarders down here, and that was just one of the many reasons. And the fireplace in the main and individual rooms kept it toasty during the cooler months."

When Reign reached out and pulled the door closed, this overwhelming feeling of love encircled and consumed her. She knew without question that her gifts were revealing the truth of Dominic's words. The people that lived here felt safe and loved, there was no denying that.

"There's so much untouched history just in this one room alone. This is amazing."

"Are you ready to go back upstairs?" Dominic asked.

"Yes," she answered with a smile. "I'm feeling a little overwhelmed right now, so this drink will definitely come in handy."

Dominic led the way and they walked in silence back through the corridor and wine cellar, then up to the library. Reign followed him feeling very content as she took everything in for a second time.

Reign was now, once again, stretched out on the plush sofa in the sitting room. But this time she was sipping the most expensive glass of wine she had ever had in her life, and it exceeded every possible expectation. And the tray of hors d'oeuvres that Dominic placed on the coffee table in front of them only enhanced every sip she took.

There were flaky mini croissants, bite sized apple turnovers, jambalaya balls, zucchini and tomato verrines, bites of candied yams and spicy steamed dumplings. Reign was in her own personal happy place, and the wine was making her even happier by the minute.

"The Quarter is so far from my mind right now you wouldn't believe it. Honestly, I'm starting to wish I didn't have to go back. I like this world you live in…you're lucky."

"Well, if it's any consolation, I need this world to keep me sane," Dominic said. "If I didn't have this, there's no way I'd be able to do what I do. I'd never be able to live with seeing people like you getting hurt daily. Fighting just to live a peaceful life."

Reign sat up straight and looked him in the eyes, "Please believe me when I say, I get it…probably more than you could possibly understand."

"Mademoiselle La'Roche, you are the most intriguing woman I've met in a long time; and this wine is nullifying any restraint I may have and intensifying my curious regard for everything that is you."

By now Dominic was sitting right next to her, and he allowed Reign's cheek to rest in his palm. While they had been in the bunker, Grace lit the logs in the fireplace, and he was now entranced by the flicker of the flames that were reflected in Reign's eyes. He wanted to kiss her, and he knew she wouldn't turn him down; he only needed to lean in and be accepting his feelings. But Dominic knew he shouldn't…couldn't. There was no possible way it would end well, no matter how right it felt.

"It's probably seventy degrees outside but fifty in here because of the air conditioning. And the lit fireplace is the oxymoron," Dominic rambled.

He was still close to her, caressing her cheek, because he couldn't bring himself to pull away. However, the perplexed look in Reign's eyes was enough to tell him he pulled her out of the moment.

"Anyway," Dominic began as he took the wine glass out of Reign's hands, "I think you've outdone yourself tonight. Maybe it's time for bed."

"Yeah, you're right," she replied. Reign knew she was lightheaded, but far from drunk, and she couldn't understand why Dominic had just passed up a perfectly good opportunity to kiss her. "And we're back to square one," she mumbled while pushing herself off the couch.

When Dominic rose to help her, she shooed him away. Maybe it was out of embarrassment, or possibly that she felt rejected, but Reign couldn't bear to look at him just yet. Her pride was too wounded.

"I can make it to the room just fine," she said from the doorway. "I'll see you in the morning," she added without a backwards glance.

Dominic stood there, watching as she walked out. The disaster he thought he'd averted now apparent in Reign's painful exit. What was he thinking? What harm could have come from a simple kiss from one who it was so apparent needed a little hope in her life. In that moment they shared, all he thought about was him and his feelings, but there were two people there. Then Dominic withdrew from the sitting room and went after her.

"Reign," he called out. He was sure her unsteady steps couldn't have carried her to her room that quickly. And that's when he felt an extreme and disturbing chill. "Reign," he called again, running toward the dining room. Then he stopped short when light from under the only locked door in the house caught his eye.

Reign left Dominic in the sitting room with as much grace as she could muster considering she was three glasses in when he'd cut her off. All she could think was: *what's wrong with me? Why is it that out of the only two men that I've ever felt drawn to, neither could bring themselves to kiss me?* She blew into her hand to smell her breath, and was relieve when there was no foul odor.

The entire time she was mulling to herself, Reign continued walking aimlessly. When she'd finally stopped, she happened to be standing in front of a door that she hadn't noticed before. Reaching down Reign, turned the knob and slowly pushed it open. She was greeted by a gentle, but penetratingly cold, breeze that caused her to shiver intensely.

Something compelled her into the room and Reign didn't have the ability to stop herself from walking in. Looking around, this area appeared to be more dated than the rest of the house.

There was something so wrong about the space, but Reign couldn't put a finger on what it was exactly. Then something to the left caught her eye as she walked further into the room. That's when she noticed a circle of candles on the floor. Reign stood there frozen in place as she discovered that the hardwood in that area was a little darker than the rest. And when she turned to run out of the room, the door slammed shut, trapping her inside.

Dominic did not want to go near that room, much less open the door. But the only thing he could think was, *what if Reign was in there. But the door is supposed to be locked*, he thought reassuringly. He always made sure that room stayed locked, especially if there were guests on the plantation; but there was light coming from within the room, so *somebody* had to be in there. Dominic took a deep breath and walked toward the door. Then, with everything in him, he turned the knob and pushed it open. Walking in, he scanned the room for anyone or anything. Then he saw her. Reign was laying on the floor, encircled with candles in the very spot where Jussie had died.

Chapter 9

Reign woke up with a start. The last thing she remembered from the previous night was…wine. A lot of wine. And finger food that was delicious enough to rival any five-star restaurant. She couldn't remember how she'd gotten into bed though, and prayed she hadn't passed out. Looking at the alarm clock she saw that it was six fifteen in the morning. Soon she'd be on her way to the Quarter, and back to reality.

Climbing out of bed Reign headed to the bathroom. She wanted one last luxurious soak in the amazing tub before leaving. And the sage soap was a thing of beauty. She had half a mind to tuck it in her purse when she left.

After twenty minutes in the tub, there was a light knock at her door.

"Yes," she answered.

"It's me," Grace called from the other side, "may I come in?"

"Of course," Reign answered.

She remained in the bathroom doorway as she spoke. "Breakfast is ready, and I've placed some clothes on the bed for you."

"Oh, thank you so much. I really wasn't expecting that," she replied. "I could've just worn what I had on yesterday."

"Nonsense. We would have had none of that. Now come, hurry so everyone can eat."

Reign regrettably ended her languid soaking and lathered her body with the sage soap. The scent engulfed her, but once her stomach growled, she was quick to rinse and dry off.

When Reign entered the dining room, Dominic, Grace, Phillipe and Gerald stood talking as they waited for her. And once she sat, they sat. She truly felt like some kind of princess, and as frivolous as it seemed, she was going to miss all of the attention.

Dominic was the first to speak.

"How did you sleep?" he asked. And though the question was innocent, something in is tone felt...tensed.

"Really well actually. You should turn this into a bed and breakfast, you'd make a killing," Reign added as she began piling food on her plate.

"You had quite a bit to drink last night. I was afraid you'd wake up cranky, or at the very least hung over."

"Nope, I feel amazing. Between that masterpiece of a bed and the oversized tub, I'd have to be happy here even on my worst day."

The remainder of the meal was quieter than previous ones, and she couldn't figure out what was wrong. Maybe the mood was somber because she was leaving, but Reign didn't give herself that much significance. They've lived all this time without her; there was no way she did anything to change their world in a day and a half.

After finishing breakfast, Reign said her goodbyes. She was sure that Grace's eyes were welling up before abruptly turning and heading back to the kitchen. Phillipe gave her a gentlemanly kiss on the back of her hand and told her to be sure to come back. And Gerald shyly, and surprisingly, gave her a warm hug before retreating to the stables. Then, just moments later, her and Dominic pulled off and she was on her way to return to city life.

The entire ride back home was quiet. It wasn't until Dominic pulled up in front of her house that he spoke.

"Even though it came out of something horrible, I'm really glad to have spent this time with you. You're wonderful company."

"If I'm such great company, why have you been so distant the whole morning and ride? You haven't said two words to me since we got in the car. Grace showed more emotion than you."

Turning, he looked at her squarely. "Something happened while you were there. Well, a few things happened, but one in particular. My entire life I've eluded any type of emotional connection with a woman. Maybe it's been purposefully, maybe not, but it's never happened. But one day with you and my life will never be the same. I don't know what to make of that."

Reign let out a pent-up sign. So he did care. And while this surprising news brought her joy, there were also a few strongly conflicting emotions. Because for all of her efforts to forget him, Krystian still meant a lot to her even with his betrayal. She wasn't sure how to handle this situation that she'd ended up in. This was completely new territory.

"Look, take this," Reign said, handing him a business card out of her wallet. "Give me a call sometime next week if you get a free moment. I'd love to give you a tour of my gallery, then maybe talk some more."

Dominic was hesitant, because he knew that anything concerning the woman sitting next to him would complicate his life immensely. But he took the card anyway, then leaned in and kissed her on the cheek.

"I'd like that a lot."

Reign climbed out of the car and gave one last look back before heading to her house. His sapphire blue eyes, midnight hair and chiseled features were ingrained in her mind. And the intensity of his appearance, she noticed, always seemed to soften up when she was near. Her life had just become so much more problematic, and that was something she really didn't need.

"I'm fine. I was considering coming in today, but maybe I shouldn't. Besides not being completely healed up just yet, I probably need some alone time," Reign said to Lisa over the phone.

"Only you know what's best. And as much as I want to wrap my hands around your neck and squeeze, I'm just glad you're ok. James was sick when he found out what happened to you."

"It's my own fault. And just like I told Alexa, it actually ended up being the time away that I needed. My life is so complicated, and being out there with Dominic on his plantation was amazing."

"Amazing? Reign what did you do?"

She laughed in response to Lisa's shocked tone and obvious assumption, "I didn't do anything. He was actually a perfect gentleman. And his home is absolutely marvelous, like nothing I've ever seen before."

"Okay, well a group just came in so I'm going to get them checked in. I'll call you later to talk about all of this amazingness."

Once the friends said their goodbyes and hung up, Reign made her way to the upstairs training room she had built more than three months prior. The entire floor had been constructed as a dojo style room, with a small corner facing the outside for her easel and art supplies. Reign had trained for over two months straight, and not once during her sessions had there been a thought that she could've been taken down by a drunkard. Her kicks and punches were precise, and consistently landed with the utmost accuracy. And as if that weren't enough, her powers themselves had increased greatly.

Reign wrapped her hands, then released all of her frustrations on the heavy bag in one corner of the room. She punched, kicked and swung until she was drenched in sweat. And after an hour, when she still hadn't regained control of her frustration, Reign removed the double hook swords from their wall mounts. She swung and sliced through the air with such intent, and it only frustrated her all the more.

Finally, after another thirty minutes, Reign stopped when it hit her. Instead of harnessing and focusing her emotions as she was trained to do, they had begun controlling her. Rage, frustration, fear…passion, it was taking control of her; and because of her abilities, the intensity of it all was penetrating.

Reign walked outside on the balcony and was immediately engulfed by a warm breeze. She remembered how, not that long ago, she was able to embrace everything about this city that she loved so much and become one with it. Now there were so many doubts and questions. She felt like now, she just knew too much.

Sitting down on the chaise, Reign breathed in heavily. All she'd ever wanted was to paint, fall in love and have one or two children. She wanted a simple and quiet life; but instead, got the exact opposite. How was she ever going to be happy becoming this other person. It also didn't help that there were now two men in her life that undoubtedly had some pull on her heart. Reign wished she had her mother or grandmother to talk to, but they wouldn't come to her. Not for something as trivial as normal life problems.

After such and intense workout and emotional influx, Reign was tired. It was only noon, but the happenings of the past weeks and months left her physically and emotionally battered and bruised. So she decided she would only close her eyes for a short while, then try to figure out what to do from there.

Staring at her on the balcony from two streets over, there was no denying the excitement she gave him. He'd been watching her for some time now, and even though Donovan had finally arrived, he continued to feed his obsession by watching her whenever he could.

Since the night he'd broken into her house Reign had taken a few security measures. This prevented him from letting himself in as he once had, even amid the blackout. He foolishly thought that triggering the power outage would gain him easy access into her home while also covering his trails. But there must have been some other power source that kept the security system engaged. Now this costly act was unfortunate for her neighbor, especially since he had no desire for anyone's blood but Reign's.

When he knocked on the kindly woman's door, she'd opened it with little caution, thinking he was just lost in the darkness and in search of directions. Her stupidity at assuming he was a harmless passerby, in conjunction with his inability to get into Reign's house, had turned him extremely violent. How dare that old lady think him harmless.

When he'd asked to come in and use the phone, she'd naively agreed. Then, when he saw the pictures of Reign on the wall, he couldn't subside his frustrations. So, in the glow of her candle lit home, he'd attacked Mrs. Renaud. He toyed with her over and over, allowing her to make it to the door, only to drag her bloodied body back. He was even kind enough to let her call the police. It must have been torture, her thinking she'd outsmarted him and made it to safety, only to be repeatedly captured. But her blood hadn't been enough, he *needed* Reign.

When she woke up, Reign was confused. She was no longer outside but in a room, and a bed, that she knew wasn't hers. Feeling around for a light, she knocked over a few things on a nearby table.

"Good morning mon cher. It is a *beautiful* day."

Reign looked at the woman who entered and tied back the heavy green curtains hanging over a large window. She seemed familiar, but Reign had no idea from where.

"We must get you dressed, the master will be leaving soon."

"Where am I?" Reign asked, running her hands gently over the green velvety soft blanket that was spread across the bed.

"Mademoiselle, are you well," the woman asked, then placed the back of her hand to Reign's forehead.

"I...I'm fine, just confused."

Reign knew that she either had to be having a dream or vision. But of what?

Climbing out of bed, Reign followed the woman's directives and got dressed. When she was finally done, she wore a simple white dress of lace and linen, and her hair was tied back into a neat bun. Walking outside the room she caught a glimpse of herself in a nearby mirror, and what she saw caused her to freeze in place. She was looking at a reflection that wasn't her own.

Smooth cocoa skin and doe eyes stared back at her; she had no clue who the woman was. Reign touched her face. Though she never experienced anything like this, she wasn't completely surprised or frightened. Reign knew there had to be a reason for what was happening to her.

"Come, hurry. He is in the stables waiting for you," the woman said, and hurried her out of the room.

Stepping out into the hallway Reign couldn't believe it. Looking around, The Eden Plantation looked just as it had when she left earlier that day. The only difference was that there were less paintings on the walls, but from what she could tell, there were plenty more people.

Walking down the grand staircase, there were people hurriedly going on about their day. And as the young French woman stood by the door waiting, it dawned on her.

"Grace?"

"Yes ma'am?" She responded.

Reign stood there staring at her for a long moment. She was breathtaking, and so full of life. Her flushed skin had a certain glow to it, and wisps of chestnut hair framed her heart-shaped face.

"You look as though you've never seen me before," Grace said after an awkward moment. "Come now, you must go to him. He's waiting for you."

Reign walked out of the house and into the direction that Grace pointed her. Looking around everything was so beautiful. There was a feeling to the plantation that the twentieth century version lacked. It was more...*alive*.

When Reign finally entered the stables, she looked curiously around. There were several beautiful and muscular stallions and mares. She was so entranced by their beauty that she didn't notice when someone approached her from behind.

"There you are. And I was beginning to think that you weren't going to come say goodbye."

Reign turned, startled, and looked up into the smoldering blue eyes of Dominic Amoureux. Well, it was him, but it wasn't. He seemed very familiar with her and his demeanor was far less guarded.

Then, after just another moment, it dawned on her. She didn't know how it was possible, but she was looking at Justine's Dominic. And he happened to be the spitting image of his great-great grandson.

"Why do you look like you've seen a ghost," he said, with a proper southern drawl.

"Oh, you just took me by surprise, that's all," she responded. If she was there, there had to be a reason for it. And convincingly playing Justine was the best way to find out what that was.

Then, when Dominic leaned down and touched his lips to hers, it felt almost natural. And it wasn't only because she was homing in on Justine's emotions either. Kissing him was something that she'd wanted to do for almost the entire time they'd been together. And now, with him holding her so close, her mind couldn't distinguish that it wasn't *her* Dominic. Their heartbeats where in sync and Reign's body felt like it was a blazing inferno.

Dominic slowly lifted his head and looked at her. His hooded eyes were so heavy with passion and excitement that she almost lost all restraint. There was a connection between him and Justine, and Reign's feelings and ability to harness and redirect emotions seemed to be intensifying everything.

"Wow Jussie, you've never kissed me like that before. Not that I have or would ever complain about your kisses, but wow."

The grin he gave her made Reign want to go in for round two.

"Now don't go looking at me like that little lady. You said you wanted to keep your virtue intact until we were wed, and that look you're giving me says otherwise. Don't give me a reason to renege on my promise."

Reign had to get her emotions in check. She had no idea why her restraint was spiraling out of control, but she had to get it together. It was way too complicated to walk in someone else's shoes while being in her own mind. And besides that, as much as the man before her looked like him, this was not two thousand sixteen Dominic. So she just looked up at his ridiculously blue eyes...and smiled.

"Come now, walk with me and Gertie so I can leave. Sooner I go, sooner I can get back to you," Dominic said, making reference to his beautiful Arabian stallion.

Reign walked Dominic to the plantation line and gave him a quick kiss before he mounted the midnight black horse.

"I'll be here waiting for you," she said, right before he turned and galloped off.

She watched him as he grew further and further in the distance. It wasn't until she couldn't see him any longer that she turned to walk back to the house. As she walked, Reign surveyed the grounds. It was so well kept and fruitful. Children laughed, men picked from apple trees, women were hanging clothes to dry and an array of people were speckled out working the land. She saw nothing but smiling faces.

Then, just as she began to climb the stairs, Reign stopped short. "No, no, no, no, no," she began quietly repeating to herself. Everything was all too familiar, and now she knew why.

Reign stepped up on the porch and took a seat on the rocking chair. *Why had she been brought to this time?* To this morbid moment when Dominic said his family had forever changed. It already happened, so she couldn't change it. Maybe there was something she was to learn.

There was so much going through Reign's mind that she was startled when Grace brought her a glass of iced tea.

"Oh, thank you," she said with a smile, taking the glass.

"Mademoiselle, is something wrong? You seem not yourself today," she asked, taking a seat in the rocking chair next to Reign.

"I'm okay Grace. It's just one of those days. Tell me, have you noticed any new faces in Eden in the last couple of weeks?"

"Why, no. Then again, I am not out here much, so I wouldn't know who is new and who is not."

Reign sipped her tea as she continued to take in her surroundings. There had to be a reason she was there, but the fact that she had no clue what it was was very frustrating.

Grace sat and relaxed just a short while longer. Dismissing herself only a few moments later, she headed off to finish putting that evening's dinner on. Reign's stomach began to growl once Grace left, and she hoped nineteen hundred and something's dinner was just as much a treat as the two thousand's.

Reign thought she would cry at the first bite of food. Everything tasted so fresh and was seasoned to perfection. She couldn't believe it was all cooked without modern conveniences. Reign was officially in her happy place; and after a nice sized serving of peach pie, she took off to sit in the private dining room.

When she walked in the cozy space everything clicked. Through some subtle probing, Reign learned that the room was used by only Justine and Dominic. They were very private about their relationship, which is likely the reason he was so surprised by her kiss earlier that day. The room had a cozy fireplace, a small polished wood table and a burgundy velvet sofa trimmed in what appeared to be mahogany.

Reign walked the perimeter of the small room, reading the titles that filled its shelves. She was in awe over the many eighteenth and nineteenth century novels, all of which were in mint condition. Then she saw it. *The Scarlett Letter* sat tucked away amid an array of many other magnificent works.

Reign gently took it off of the shelf and walked to the couch where she stretched out to read by the fireplace.

She was about eight chapters in when Reign heard a light thump. She wasn't sure where it had come from, but she knew something was wrong. Getting up off of the sofa Reign walked toward the door, but was surprised when it flew open and a strong gust of wind pushed her back. Looking up from where she'd fallen on the floor, she saw five female intruders, all of which stared at her in distain.

Each of them had fiery red hair that hung down their backs. And once they'd entered, the door slammed closed.

"What do you want?" Reign asked, attempting to stall.

None of them bothered to answer her, but one who appeared to be the leader spoke, "ligatis manibus eius."

Reign had barely blinked when she found herself bound to one of the dining table chairs and gagged. She watched as the five women began what looked to be a ritualistic act, speaking in a language that was vaguely familiar. And when they sliced their hands open, allowing the blood to drip over the fireplace flame, Reign felt her lungs constrict. Then, just before blacking out from lack of oxygen, Reign saw the dining room door swing open and Dominic walk in.

The next time Reign opened her eyes she was laying on the floor in the center of the candles, cold and unable to move.

"Libri quinque in hoc lumen, quid nobis et tibi est, iube haec perferri sitque... libri quinque in hoc lumen, quid nobis et tibi est, iube haec perferri sitque..."

Reign heard them chanting over and over, but she didn't understand a word of what they were saying. As she lay there shivering, Reign was finally able to open her eyes and attempt to focus. When she looked up, she could see that the women had formed a circle around her, and their skin…it was as red as their hair.

Her thoughts were so muddled. She wanted to sit up, she *needed* to get up. And as Reign's hands moved ever so slightly with the little strength she had, she could tell she was laying in something sticky. Then she remembered Dominic's story. *I'm lying in my own blood*, she thought to herself. And the women, their skin hadn't turned red; they were covered in her blood.

Reign somehow knew what she had to do, and with one last deep breath looked over to where Dominic sat, helplessly bound to the chair. Their eyes met, and in that moment she knew she had to let him see how much she loved him. How much her heart was breaking, knowing what needed to be done.

"Mimi kupita juu na wewe kuelimisha huu. Zawadi hii, yangu yote, sasa ni lenu," were words Reign did not know, but were said with her final breath.

Chapter 10

When Reign opened her eyes, she was once again laying across the chaise on her balcony. She realized she must have been out of it for some time, because the sun was beginning to hang low in the sky. Still groggy and attempting to wrap her head around what she had just witnessed, Reign pushed herself up and made her way downstairs.

She was hungry, but since she really hadn't been sleep, Reign was also exhausted. So she opted to make a not so time consuming sandwich and a salad. At that moment all she truly wanted was to get some real sleep.

Sitting at the island, Reign tried to remember everything she could about the vision in between bites. Just like when she'd had the vision of her grandparents, there had to be a reason for this one.

Reign was on her last bite of sandwich when the phone rang.

"Hey you," she greeted her father.

"You know I was in a panic over you until Alexa called yesterday. Why didn't you call me child?"

"I lost my phone. The only number I remembered was Alexa's. Maybe you should stop changing yours so much."

"I am happy to see you safe and home. And what of this detective man that saved you. And why should you need saving at all? Your gifts should have grown greatly by now."

Reign gave a light laugh, "Mô pé, one question at a time please. As far as my gifts...I don't know. I tried to use them, but it was like they fizzled out. And even with all of the training, all I could do was panic and flail like a dying chicken."

Reign paused, trying to figure out how to tell her father about Dominic. Especially since mentioning him meant she had to also tell Julien of Mrs. Renaud's *murder*.

"And this man?" Julien urged her on when he sensed hesitation.

"I initially met him Tuesday night when..." Reign drifted off because she couldn't bear to say it.

"Mô fiy, continue. When what?"

She waited just a little longer before continuing, "There was a blackout on this side Tuesday evening. He came knocking on my door about Mrs. Renaud." Reign stopped for a second when she heard her father's breath catch, then continued, "Someone broke in and murdered her. Dad, she's gone and I feel like somehow it's my fault."

"It is not your fault. You did nothing to deserve any of this. If anything, you are the most innocent of everyone. I know it breaks your heart that Mrs. Renaud is gone, but she was a good woman with a beautiful spirit. She is at peace now."

"You're right, but I hate knowing that my life is linked to her death," Reign said after a moment.

"So," Julien continued, not wanting to allow his daughter to continue succumbing to her pain at losing another loved one, "you say Mr. Detective questioned you, but how did you get to his house."

"First, his name is Dominic, and secondly…I don't know. I guess he happened to be around when I was being attacked. Honestly, I barely remember any of it. But I do know if he hadn't been there, I'd probably be dead. And for good this time," Reign concluded, inwardly daring her father to question Dominic's motives.

"And you say you trust him…this Dominic?" Julien asked.

"Well, I owe him my life. I owe him everything."

Father and daughter were silent on the phone for a moment. It was as though they were both quietly reassuring the other that they were alive and well. Then the moment was interrupted by an incoming call from Alexa.

"Hey, I have to go. Lex is calling. I'll check in with you another day though, because I'm definitely calling it a night early tonight."

"Mo linm twa."

"I love you too."

Then Reign ended that call only to start another one with Alexa.

"Hey. What's up?"

"I just wanted to check on you and see if you were up for a dinner party tomorrow evening? I know it's last minute, but I thought the idea of getting everyone together would bbe good."

Reign didn't much feel like being around any one. Her run in the other night still left her angry. She couldn't ever remember feeling so helpless despite being so strong. But Reign knew she couldn't brush off the people in her life forever. After all, they were the ones she was doing all of this for.

"I think I can make some free time," she answered.

"Great, because after everything that's happened, it would be really wonderful just to be normal for a bit," Alexa replied.

I'll never be normal again, Reign thought to herself, but refrained from saying. "Yeah, it would be great. So what time should I be there?"

"Come around five thirty."

After saying their goodbyes, Reign hung up the phone and headed to her room. She didn't want a vision, dream, or to be teleported back in time. All she wanted was an uninterrupted and peaceful good night's sleep. She'd deal with everything else in the morning.

When Reign woke, the bright morning sun was high in the sky. She knew she had a full day ahead of her, but still she wanted to take some leisure time and shop for an outfit for that evening's dinner party. So, she climbed out of bed, showered and dressed then was off to start her day.

The first thing Reign had in mind was to get her hair done. Overall her long and curly locks were easy to maintain, but she wanted someone else to fuss over it for a change. Then, after a wash and bone straight blow out, she headed to Riverwalk for an outfit.

Reign was always so engulfed in her world or art, up until recently, and never really took the time to shop the outlet. Of course a good deal was always right up her alley, but she tended to avoid throngs of people. And as unsettling as her life currently was, even though she would have much rather done some closet boutique shopping, she braved the Saturday crowds.

Weaving in and out of running children, primping moms, and picky teens for two hours had Reign on her last functioning nerve. All she wanted was a dress, and that was quickly becoming the task of all tasks. It wasn't until she was about to call it quits that Reign spotted a store that appeared to have just the kinds of clothes she was looking for.

Entering the quaint little retailer, she was immediately greeted by the scent of saffron and lemon. It was as odd combination, but she found it to be quite calming. As Reign leisured through the store, a soft-spoken associate approached her.

"Good afternoon. Did you need help finding anything?"

Reign was about to say no, but then thought better of it.

"I need something to wear for a dinner party tonight. Sexy, sophisticated but a little flirty. Something that other women would want to be jealous of me in, but couldn't because it's so amazing," Reign answered with a light laugh.

The associate took a second to consider her client's request, then stepped away with a bright smile. The two-piece ensemble she brought back was every bit of what Reign was looking for. The skirt was long, black, ankle length and sported a thigh high slit. The top was a black sheer bodysuit with strategically placed bands in zaffre blue which wrapped around it from front to back.

Reign took the hanger then looked at the associate's name badge. "Amyrah. That's such a pretty name, and thank you. This is perfect."

"Thank you. I can ring you out now if you're ready."

Nodding and heading to the checkout counter, Reign stopped short when something caught her eyes. It was a full hooded black bodysuit. Having no idea why, or where she would wear it, she took it from the rack and added it to her purchase.

Feeling accomplished, Reign decided her next mission would be lunch. She hadn't eaten anything for breakfast, and it seemed that as her powers grew, so did her appetite. However, on her way out of the huge shopping complex, she was drawn to a free-standing booth in the center aisle.

The sign name read *Devereux's Blades and Daggers*. She was unsure why she was compelled to pay the slender man behind the counter a visit. In all honestly, the mere look of him made her uncomfortable.

"Bonne après-midi belle dame. Comment puis-je vous aider?"

"Oh, I'm sorry. My French isn't that great. Parlez vous anglais?" Reign responded to the clerk.

"Oui, mademoiselle. What can I do for you?" he answered in a heavy French accent.

As Reign walked closer to him, she could see a hint of yellow shimmering off his body. The closer she got the more intense the yellow became, then she realized what was it was. Reign could see his aura. This was something she was never able to do before, but now amid her discomfort, the gift became apparent. Her apprehension diminished and she gave him a bright smile as she continued to approach the counter.

"Honestly, I don't know. I was on my way out and I saw your booth. Just curious I guess."

"Très bien. You may look."

Reign strolled around the circular glass encasement where an assortment of knives and daggers had been secured. There were so many sizes, colors and blade types; but they were all remarkable. Then, once Reign had almost completed her survey of the display she saw it. A black dagger with a slightly curved handle and dual tips that came to a sharp point. As she examined the mirroring tips of the blade, Reign could tell that it was extremely sharp.

"Would you like to see it closer?" the man asked.

Reign was not aware that she'd been staring at the dagger with such interest, "Yes, please."

First, he gave her a glove to put on. "To protect yourself from getting cut," he answered before she could question him.

Once Reign had it on, he handed her the knife. She thought it would weigh more, but it was surprisingly light. Then the man pressed a button on its handle and the curved blade of the dagger quickly folded back into itself.

"Oh wow!"

"It is a formidable blade, and can be a deadly weapon in the right hands."

Reign didn't need much convincing. She purchased the glove, dagger and a thigh strap. The next time anyone attempted to put their hands on her, she was going to be prepared in as many ways as she possibly could be.

Chapter 11

After a day of pampering, expected and unexpected purchases, and some much-needed fresh air, Reign decided to finally head home. Truthfully, there was a lot on her mind and she was clueless on how to address any of it.

As she sped down the Pontchartrain Expressway with the windows down, music blasting and wind flying through her hair, she glanced over at the bag in the passenger's seat that contained her newly purchased weapon. Reign knew the recent attack was what prompted the purchase; she had no intention of ever feeling as helpless as she had that night.

By the time she reached highway ten, Reign's thoughts had shifted to the somewhat love triangle she'd found herself in with Krystian and Dominic. Two very similar but different men that left her rethinking life.

Krystian was such an all-around good guy, but there were obvious flaws when it came to him. Not to mention the fact that his father wanted her dead. But when she looked into his eyes, Reign could feel the intensity of his affections for her. She wanted to trust and believe him, but wasn't willing to risk it given the fact that he couldn't actually control what his father did or didn't do.

Then there was Dominic. She'd only known him for a very short while, but that seemed to be the theme of her life lately. The less time she knows a person, the greater the connection to them. And her connection with Dominic was confusing and unexplainable. His mannerisms and presence was like something straight out of a romance novel, and it was quickly drawing her in.

When Reign exited off onto Governor Nicholls, her phone rang.

"Hello Mr. Peyreux," she answered with a smile.

"Good afternoon to you too my lovely one," her father answered.

"And to what do I owe the pleasure of this call?"

This time last year Julien hadn't spoken to his daughter in almost three years, and she had had every intention on keeping it as such. She'd wanted nothing to do with her hoodoo doing voodoo practicing father, and it hurt him immensely. He was glad that his only child was back in his life, but the cost to have it so was one Reign had paid dearly.

"Well," Julien began, knowing the news he had to share with her would add to her already heavy burden, "when you told me of how you couldn't use your powers the night you were attacked, I became concerned. It's one thing to have limited strength because you're still learning, but to have none at all, that shouldn't be. We are the power that we hold, so to be nonexistent at any given moment is not possible."

"What did you find out?" she asked him calmly, but inside was screaming for answers.

"I used every tool I had to try and understand what was happening, but it wasn't until it happened to me that I understood."

"Wait, what? It happened to you too?"

"Yes," Julien answered. "Since we last spoke I decided to ward the house from Nicola. At least this way, her access to my power would be nonexistent here. Doing this takes a great deal of focus and energy, so partway through I did not notice when she broke past the shallow veil that had begun to form."

"She broke through the warding?!" Reign asked in utter shock, because her father was still extremely powerful.

"Well, not really. I wasn't finished, so she snuck in…like through a door that is still cracked open."

Reign calmed down at his explanation. Knowing she was nowhere near her father's strength at the moment left her weary of a run-in Nicola. But Julien assured her that she would be advanced beyond him once mastering her gifts; and this gave her hope that she could take on her great-great grandmother if it came to that.

"What I found out was that my strength, even though it remained, drained slightly in her presence…like she was feeding off of me. So, for someone like you, strong but untrained, she could have taken you down to nothing."

Reign's hands grew icy as she pulled up in front of her house and parked. The mere thought that Nicola was around or had anything to do with her attack left her cold. How could someone that was supposed to love her by all natural standards be so hell bent on her death?

"Well, that makes sense, because the first try only left my hands warm. The second try I was completely empty. Paer, can I ward my house too?"

"You can, but you're just not strong enough yet. And since it's your home, so you have to perform the warding by your magic alone."

"You always call with great news," Reign said sarcastically. "From now on anytime I see your name pop up, I'm pressing the ignore button."

Julien gave a small chuckle from the other end, "It is part of my talent."

"Okay, well I'm just getting home and I need to start getting ready for Lex's dinner party."

"Okay. Well, remember to keep with the spirit trainings. And I also think it's time that we begin the legacy rights."

Julien was speaking of the three ceremonies that would pass down the collective ancestral powers from parent to child. What Reign had now were gifts that were her own and promised to her from conception, which was only part of her abilities. Once all three spirit ceremonies were completed, everything already in her would quadruple.

"So soon?" she asked. "Because I'm not even close to ready for that level of strength."

"Yes mon amour. We don't have time to ease you in to this. Once Nicola is grounded on the physical plain, she will give you no warning."

Reign knew he was right no matter how much she wanted to deny it. Her time was winding down, but she was terrified that she'd lose all sense of the woman she once was.

"Ok well, while I'm still normal, I'm going to go take a long bath and then get dressed for my best friend's party. Thank you for the info too. I love you so much."

"I love you too shé, and we will talk tre bento," Julien said, hesitant to get off of the phone.

"I'll be fine. I promise," Reign assured him. Then getting out of the car, she reached back to grab the bag that contained her new dagger.

"Okay okay, au revoir mô shé. Have fun."

Much to her surprise, Reign found a package on her doorstep when she arrived home. Unfortunately, in light of recent events, she was just as concerned that it may have been a weapon of mass destruction as the possibility of it being a gift from a suiter. So, she was happy and relieved when she saw that the note taped to its side had shown it was from Dominic.

A short while later Reign was languorously soaking in the tub that was scented with the sage oil that was a part of the gift set from Dominic. There was also sage: soap, lotion, shampoo and conditioner. He'd given her the same gift set in jasmine and sandalwood as well. Reign had made a mental note to call and thank him for his thoughtfulness.

By now she had been in the tub so long that her fingers and toes were beginning to wrinkle, but was still unenthusiastic about getting out. Reign felt like she was floating on a carefree cloud and did not want to be snapped back into her complicated reality. But time was ticking away, and she would have to head out to Alexa's in just over an hour.

"Up and at em kiddo," she mumbled while reluctantly climbing out of the still warm water.

She truly was looking forward to spending time with her friends, but her mini *vacation* had her apprehensive about seeing Krystian. Being near him while she was still so vulnerable didn't seem like the best move to make at the moment, though she was left with little choice.

Finally dressed in the new outfit, her curly mane now bone straight and hanging down her back, she sparingly misted herself with a cherry blossom body splash.

Reign looked at her reflection in the floor length mirror. Minus the slowly fading bruise on her forehead that was still evident from the attack, she looked perfect.

"This should be fun," she said to herself, then grabbed her purse and headed out the door.

Krystian was on edge the entire day. For some reason the thought of seeing Reign left him anxious. It was a ridiculous feeling to have, especially now that she was at least cordial to him. How could one woman be so maddening?

"You ok Krys?" Adrian asked while watching his friend pace the living room floor of their condo.

"Do I *look* ok?" he replied with obvious cynicism.

"Look, if you're going to be in your feelings tonight about Reign, maybe you should skip it."

Krystian stopped pacing and stared at him. "Besides the fact that it wouldn't happen anyway, you know the many other reasons that *can't* happen."

"I assume you mean Nathan?" Adrian questioned emphatically.

"Isn't that the most obvious? This must be done tonight, especially since Reign and I are at least on speaking terms. If I don't and she finds out later, everything could blow up in my face. In *our* faces," he finished pointedly.

At that moment, Alexa emerged from one of the upstairs bedrooms and descended the staircase. Adrian looked her way and didn't take his eyes off of her as she made her way to him.

"You look incredible," he said, admiring the way the crimson of the gown complimented her golden honey colored skin.

"No, *we* look amazing," she replied, correcting him.

And less than an hour later, guests began arriving. Alexa made sure the bar had been fully stocked, and even hired someone to tend it. The overall feel was that of an open bar at an event, which was exactly what she was going for.

There were about twelve other people besides Adrian, Alexa and Krystian mingling by the time Reign had arrived. And when she walked in, there were plenty of curious glances that strayed her way, though there were obvious attempts at being inconspicuous.

"Bonsoir ma soeur. Je suis si heureuse de te voir. Voulez-vous prendre un verre?"

"Lex, you know my French is not the best," Reign said smiling, "but yes, a glass of wine would be amazing."

The two friends walked to the bar area to chit chat for a few minutes. A few minutes passed before Reign looked away and happened to notice Krystian in the corner of the room. She was unsure why, but something seemed off about him. It looked like him, but it didn't *feel* like him. And, as one of the newer gifts that was revealed to her was reading auras, his appeared to be very dark. And it wasn't until he made eye contact with her that Reign turned away.

"Two glasses of the Riesling," Alexa said to the bartender. "Now, tell me what's going on with you?"

"Nothing much, just trying to wrap my head around an entirely new life. I spoke to my father yesterday about the night I was attacked. He has this theory that Nicola was probably near and intentionally drained me."

"Wait, she can do that?" Alexa asked in disbelief.

"Apparently, she can," Reign answered after taking a sip from her glass. "I have no idea how it's even possible though, because she can't take from me until she's drained my father."

"Like literally drained his powers completely?" Alexa asked.

"No, it's more complicated than that. In my line, we consist of two sources of magick: what we were born with and what we inherit. She can only tap into and leach from the inherited part, which is why dad's theory is so confusing to me. I'm receiving dormant powers, I haven't begun to get inherited ones yet."

Reign and Alexa were so deep in their conversation that they did not realize when the man that had been eyeing them for the past few moments finally headed their way.

"Hello. I'm so sorry for intruding, but I had to come over and speak. You must be Reign?" he asked, with his hand outstretched.

She placed her glass on the bar and looked at him, confused and a little annoyed. "So, you're taking this 'starting over' thing pretty serious I see."

The man looked back at her and grinned, "Ah, I see my brother hasn't told you yet."

"Maybe we should begin seating for dinner," Alexa interjected nervously.

"No, wait. What are you talking about?" Reign asked, clasping Alexa's wrist before she had the chance to walk away.

Just then, another man walked over and joined them in their conversation. Reign did a double take, because she couldn't believe what she was seeing. Two men who looked exactly like one another were standing in front of her. And the most disturbing part was, they both looked exactly like Krystian.

"Reign, I'm so sorry for his presumption. This is my twin brother, Nathan."

Reign looked at, who she guessed, was Krystian, "So can I assume by the way Alexa was trying to get away that everyone knew this but me?"

"If by everyone you mean her, Adrian and Lisa, then yes," Krystian answered.

Reign looked at Nathan. Appearance wise he looked exactly like his brother, but his presence was different. His energy was disturbing her spirit in a most intense way.

"Well, it's nice to meet you Reign. I'm so sorry it was done this way though. I'd rather you had known who I was when I introduced myself," Nathan said.

Taking his extended hand, she shook it and gave him a halfhearted smile. "Well, you probably should have checked with your brother *before* deciding to walk over here then. That would have been the most thoughtful thing to do," she responded, then turned and walked away.

"She is something, like *really* something. I can see why you have a thing for her," Nathan said when it was just him and Krystian standing there.

"Do you not know when to stop? Or maybe that filter between your brain and mouth needs to be repaired," Krystian said to his brother while walking to the dinner table where the rest of the guests were gathering. "I really need you to get it together. You don't know these people, and I really would prefer it if you didn't make a spectacle."

"Now, when have I ever made a spectacle? And that Donovan thing was so long ago it should be considered ancient."

As Reign went to take her seat she noticed Lisa for the first time that evening, who was accompanied by James. They were so focused on their conversation that they didn't notice her at all. She smiled a bit and thought to herself, *and out of my imminent danger blossoms the great fabled love story*.

"I'm so sorry I didn't tell you about Nathan," Alexa said, taking the seat beside her friend. "I wanted to give Krystian the chance to make introductions..."

"And we see how well *that* turned out," Reign interrupted.

"Look, he came knocking on Krystian's door while you were on your romantic getaway and could not be found. You need to let it go."

"Oh, you're referring the romantic getaway with the man who rescued me from rape and possibly murder?" Reign retorted under her breath.

Alexa paused, immediately aware that she had gone too far. "I'm sorry. That was uncalled for," but she stopped talking when Adrian sat down next to her.

"It's really good to see you. You had everyone worried sick about you," he said to Reign, unaware of the escalating conversation he interrupted between her and his fiancée.

Reign gave him a smile, then directed her attention to the man that now sat directly across from her. Most probably couldn't tell the difference between Krystian and his brother, but she could. The man now looking back at her was Nathan, and she knew it was him because his aura read so dark...almost pitch black. And the way he looked at her was unlike any way Krystian ever had. There was something about Nathan that did not sit well with Reign, but she couldn't put her finger on what it was.

Dinner was painfully long. Krystian's attempts at avoiding her were quite apparent, while his brother had taken every opportunity to get her attention. And even though she was in the presence of her two closest friends, it wasn't the same since they both became involved. Reign had never known that fifth wheel feeling until now.

Between dinner and dessert, Reign had gotten up and headed to the restroom. On her way there, she nearly collided with Krystian in the hallway. Aware of how obvious he'd been about avoiding her, she excused herself and continued on her way.

"Reign wait, can I talk to you for a second?"

Surprised when he spoke to her, she kept her unbothered appearance intact.

"We've been in the same room for hours and you barely acknowledge me, but now you want to talk?"

She looked at him intently for a moment, and when he did not continue, Reign turned on her heel and continued toward the bathroom. However, she did not expect it when Krystian reached out and clasped her wrist. His hold was gentle enough that she knew if she pulled away, he'd let her go. Reign stopped, then turned and looked up at him.

"I'm sorry. So much of what's happening is my fault and I don't know how to fix it," he began.

"I don't know what it is you want from me, because I certainly can't tell you how to fix it. You have all of these secrets, but I told you the truth even when I knew you'd think

I was crazy. I thought I was protecting you, but you ended up being the one I needed protection *from*."

"Now that's kind of extreme. You never needed protection from me."

"Didn't I? I wasn't attacked until I met you. And you yourself said that your only intention for me was to ruin your father's plans. It wasn't until you met me that things changed. You hate him so much; you don't know what you would have been willing to do had we not actually met."

Krystian stood there staring at her speechlessly. He couldn't deny she was right. His hate for Donovan had superseded everything at one point. But that changed the day he met Reign. In frustration he ran his hands across his face.

"You're right. Everything you said is true, but it changed the very first time I met you. After that initial night we met I wished Adrian had never talked me into that date, because I knew that *by any means necessary* was no longer an option."

Reign continued to stare at him. There were still feelings there. Intense, unresolved and deep feelings that she couldn't possibly deny. Looking at him, with frustration on his face and misery in his eyes, spoke to her more than any of his words ever could. Her life had become ten times more complicated in just a matter of minutes.

He finally let go of her wrist, the raised his hand and caressed her cheek. "You've done something to me. I've never felt like this for anyone ever. Everything about you floods my mind and consumes me and we've never even kissed."

The hallway was dim and the chatter and clank of dishes seemed so distant as they stood there staring at one another. They were having a moment, and it was as intense and unforgiving as hurricane Katrina. Emotions swam in both their eyes, but who would make the first move?

"There you are Krys. I was looking for you," Nathan said after he'd entered the hallway. "Samantha and her friend asked us to go to some bar with them after we left here. They're really into handsome twins," he continued, followed by a wink.

When he heard his brother's voice, Krystian turned his head. He was caught off guard by Nathan's intrusion on whatever was just happening between him and Reign.

"I don't..." he began, turning to look back at Reign, but she was gone. "Yeah, fine," he finished.

Krystian looked back in the direction Reign had gone before heading out toward the dining area. Why did things have to be so tense between them? There had to be a way for him to fix it before it was too late.

Chapter 12

It was nearly nine o'clock by the time Reign arrived home. She had no clue what to make of her night. Between Alexa making light of her near-death experience and her close encounter with Krystian, she was more than happy to be home and away from everyone.

Krystian. How could she want to kiss and choke someone in the same breath? When Nathan had interrupted their much-needed conversation, it almost felt like he had done so intentionally. But that made no sense at all. Reign didn't know him from a hole in the wall, so why would he take time to bother with her.

Reign dropped her keys on the entryway table, kicked off her shoes, laid across the couch and turned on the TV. She didn't have the energy to change just yet. All she wanted was to do absolutely nothing. Krystian gave as much energy as he took from her and it was exhausting, especially now that her ability to read auras was apparent. Reign was left feeling like she'd been consumed by his intensity, and oddly enough, she wanted to be. But he needed to get it together; she couldn't continue going back and forth with him.

Just as she had finally decided on a show there was a knock at the door. She laid there for a minute, tempted to pretend like she was either not home or asleep, but quickly changed her mind. With all that was going on lately that wouldn't have been the wisest of decisions. With her luck, it was probably someone with a life or death emergency.

"Just a sec," Reign called out as she rolled off the couch.

Still in her evening wear, she made it to the door and peeked out of the sidelight. Her heart raced a little when she saw Dominic on the other side. He stood there in black jeans and a white button up, and the sight of him caused her breath to catch.

"Hey, is everything okay?" Reign asked after opening the door.

"Yeah," he answered with a heavy sigh. "I passed by earlier but you weren't here. Do you mind if I come in for a minute?"

"Sure, come on," she replied, stepping aside to let him in. "What's going on?"

Dominic didn't say a word until they were both seated on the couch. He looked like he was pained and in deep thought. "So, you know I've been working on Mrs. Renaud's case, right?"

Reign wasn't prepared for this conversation, not after the night she'd had. And she wanted to tell him just that, but didn't. "Yes, I know."

"Well, for the past few days I've been sorting through evidence and what not," he paused, looking like he didn't want to continue.

"Go on."

"From everything I could gather, it appears the intruder was initially after you."

Reign's face paled as she stared at him in disbelief. The alarming news had her grasping to get her thoughts together. It wasn't necessarily a shock that someone was after her. What bothered Reign was the fact that now she officially knew it was her fault that Mrs. Renaud was dead.

"How could you tell?"

"The morning I dropped you off something didn't feel right. Everything just felt...off. So, I came back later with every intention of asking you if I could sweep your property, but you weren't here," Dominic said, then looked directly into her eyes. "I hope you don't mind, but I did it anyway. I needed to follow up on my suspicion."

"And did you find anything?"

"Well, I brought a police dog with me. He picked up the scent of Mrs. Renaud's intruder over here as well. Oh, and I found this."

He reached in his pocket and pulled out a silver lock pick inside a little baggie. As Reign stared at it she realized she had been right about the feeling that someone was near or watching her.

"It appears that when he couldn't get in here, he went to your neighbor's. It's almost like he wanted to make sure you were somehow tied into this."

Dominic gave Reign a second to take everything in before continuing.

"Do you know *why* he couldn't get in? I have to assume this wasn't random, especially with the power failure and him being so well prepared."

Reign paused for a minute to consider just how honest she wanted to be. Although she trusted Dominic, she wasn't sure just how much she should confide in him. Then there was also the possibility that she could be putting his life in danger by telling him anything.

Taking a deep breath, Reign began. "A few months ago, someone broke into my house while I was out. It got a little messy and I never found out who it was, but upping my security system became priority."

"Did you file a report?"

"No. Honestly it seemed pointless," Reign replied. And when it looked like Dominic was going to reprimand her for her lack of action, she put her hand up to stop him. "There's a *lot* about me that you don't know. My life is…complicated, and to tell you a little would mean I'd have to tell you everything. Just please trust me when I say my way was better."

Dominic was no stranger to secrets and the effect they can have on everyone involved. He wanted to trust Reign's judgment, but the protectiveness he felt for her would not allow him to let it go. More than a few times since the night of her attack Dominic would get a flash of her bruised and bloodied face. He didn't want to imagine what would have happened to her had he not been there.

"Maybe it would be easier to trust your judgment if I hadn't saved your life less than a week ago because you decided to walk home alone."

Reign was stumped. The way her life was now set up, secrets shared were either all or nothing. Even though she wasn't quite ready to put herself out there again, Dominic questioning her judgment did not sit well with her.

"I know," she began, resting her hand on his cheek, "please believe me I do. You have quite literally been my superman, and I owe you my life. I want nothing more than to tell you every secret, every happening, every*thing*…and in time, I will. But that time cannot be now."

It wasn't until that moment, when Reign was but a few inches from his face, that Dominic noticed her attire. The long split left one leg exposed, her hair was straight and a little tousled from lying on the sofa, and those amber eyes were made even more intense by the dark makeup she chose.

Reign felt the air change the moment his thoughts drifted. It was like millions of particles all around them had been charged and radiated off of their skin. They both sat there, caught in the moment but unmoving by the secrets they harbored.

Dominic stirred first, sitting up and shifting himself from her touch. "You know whoever did this will be back right? Whoever it was came with a purpose, which was you; and they won't stop until they have you."

"I know. Actually, I've always known. This is a part of that, *I want to tell you everything but I can't just yet*, thing," Reign responded, then stood up and headed to the fridge.

Being so close to Dominic was interfering with her judgment *and* her hormones. She needed a cold shower, but a cold drink would have to suffice for now.

Reign was taking a long drink of water and did not feel when Dominic entered the kitchen. After placing her glass in the sink, she was startled at seeing his lean frame relaxed against the wall. He smiled at her attempt to recover herself before speaking.

"As much as I know you sharing any information would help with all of this mess, I'm a man of my word. I won't try to convince you to change your mind. I know you'll share as much or as little as you want when you're ready. However, I do need you to know that I am going to protect you…even if that means camping outside your door at random hours."

Dominic was just as bad as Krystian. She had no idea why these two men were so determined to risk themselves to keep her safe. But at least Krystian knew *almost* everything, including the fact that she did have the ability to protect herself. Whereas Dominic just thought she was a hapless damsel.

"You know that's not…."

"Don't tell me it's not necessary. Your neighbor is murdered only because someone couldn't get to you. Then you tell me your house has been broken into before. And let's not forget that I literally rescued you from who knows what only days ago."

Reign knew he was right. Without him knowing anything, he came up with the most logical conclusions. She was frustrated, and being around him was making her stir crazy. Reign was not in a place emotionally to be around anyone she was even remotely attracted to.

Walking away from the sink, she tried to sidestep him and head back into the living room, but something was wrong. She took three steps and was only inches from him, when she froze. The air became so thick and cold that Reign started to shiver. Looking up, her vision was hazy and she could barely make out Dominic's face.

Her strength was quickly draining, but she was able to utter two words before collapsing against Dominic. Two words that he would not understand, but meant everything to Reign, "She's here."

Chapter 13

Dominic stood there, Reign limp in his arms, in shock and panic. He was in a sudden state of alarm not because she'd collapsed, but because her body felt so cold. And, much to his confusion, she felt like she was getting colder by the second. Something was terrifyingly wrong and he doubted there was anything he could do to fix it.

Scooping Reign up in his arms, Dominic carried her to the bedroom and laid her down. He felt so completely helpless as he took the throw from the foot of the bed and covered her with it. He didn't know any of her family or friends or what was wrong to even begin helping her. And what did she mean by, *she's here*?

He could see the slow rise and fall of her chest as she lay on the bed, seemingly unaffected the sudden drop of her body temperature. Dominic placed the back of his hand on her forehead and was met with an unnatural coldness. Taking a deep breath, he made a decision.

"I can't lose you," he whispered in her ear. "So, if exposing myself means saving your life, then so be it."

Without missing a beat Dominic removed his shoes, kneeled on the side of the bed and placed his hands on Reign's where they rested on her chest. He was going to harness an ancient magick that had been bequeathed to him for safe keeping, and this would allow him to take a glimpse inside Reign's mind and gauge her condition. Closing his eyes and began to focus intently until he could finally feel her presence.

Reign was having an intense moment of déjà vu and it was annoying. Her great grandmother was anything but original and it was becoming so anti-climactic that Reign almost felt bad. As in previous visions, it was dark and cold and the faint smell of sulfur lingered.

She began walking and was met with a familiar crunch underfoot. Reign had to admit though, the blinding emptiness would have struck fear into her very core had it not been for the hours of meditation she'd recently endured. She may not have met her full potential just yet, but she was strong, and refused to cower before one so evil and hate filled.

"I know you're here Nicola. This whole thing reeks of you. So what threat do you have for me now?"

All Reign could hear was the echo of her own voice and the emptiness that reverberated with each step. Then the blackness started to break until it felt like dusk under a moonlit night.

"You are becoming quite bold," a voice said from the darkness.

"Did you think that I wouldn't be?" Reign questioned. "I mean, no matter how much you try to deny me, I am still your blood."

"Child, you mistake my intentions. It is *because* we are bonded that I *can* do this. Your natural power was foretold to surpass us all, and our shared blood is the reason I *will* strip you of these gifts."

Reign laughed lightly before addressing the woman who was beginning to become more and more obnoxious as opposed to threatening.

"You can *try* to syphon my legacy magick but you cannot steal natural gifts, no matter how much you may lack in your own."

Reign could see Nicola's form begin to emerge from the darkness. If she were to be honest with herself, the old woman did look stronger...even younger. But none of it mattered to Reign, Nicola was still the reason for much of her family's pain.

Looking at her great grandmother Reign's anger suddenly became explosive until she started to feel an intense heat emanating from her hands. She was finally doing it. Reign had unintentionally harnessed the rage she was feeling, and now the manifestation of it was shown by the iridescent flames that radiated from her fingertips.

"This is good. Soon you will be ripe and ready for plucking, and no one will be able to stop me."

Reign was thrown off guard when Nicola reached out and clasped the back of her neck.

"So you've brought someone with you," Nicola stated matter of factly, her amethyst eyes reflective of her rage. "We don't take kindly to peeping toms around these parts," she continued, then waved her hand as if swatting a fly. "Hmmm, this one is very strong."

"Now I know you're crazy. A ghost seeing ghosts," Reign said. "And I would appreciate it if you would *let go of me!*" She added with much emphasis.

Nicola had been so distracted by the lurking stranger that she was not prepared when Reign focused still flaming fingers in her direction. There was an explosion of light when her hands made contact with Nicola, and then there was nothing.

Dominic opened his eyes as he continued to kneel on the floor. He was having a hard time comprehending what he'd just seen. Reign was definitely harboring secrets, and she was *much* more than what she appeared to be. Looking down when she took a deep breath, Dominic could feel her hands begin to warm up.

"Hey you," he said when her eyes fluttered opened, "you scared me."

Reign was so groggy, but she was completely aware of everything she'd just experienced with Nicola. However, she had no knowledge of where she was physically or who was talking to her.

"Where am I?" Reign asked, trying to sit up.

Dominic reached over and turned on the nightstand lamp. When the light clicked on Reign instinctively covered her eyes.

"Open them slowly," he instructed, still kneeling in front of her. "You were out of it for a while."

She took a deep breath, lowered her hands, then gradually opened her eyes and focused them on Dominic. What he saw almost knocked the wind out of him. Reign's eyes were almost translucent, like uncut diamonds. All he could do was stare at her as, nerve by nerve, her eyes slowly regained their amber color.

"I'm so sorry. I hope I didn't scare you," she said, thinking that his shocked expression was due to her recent *episode*. "I'm okay though. This has been happening a lot lately, but it's nothing to worry about."

He knew that she was not ready to tell him anything, and to reveal what he had seen would likely do more damage than good. Although now he was even more intrigued with her than he had been. But it wasn't her obvious physical power that drew him in; it was the strength that radiated from her core and made her the person she was that continued to call to him.

"No, it's okay. I mean yes, you collapsing into my arms threw me off for a second," Dominic replied with a smile, "but it wasn't anything I couldn't handle."

Reign looked at the clock and saw it read eleven thirty-two. "You've been here over two hours," she stated.

"Yeah, well besides the obvious reason for my visit and your epic swoon, I figure it as time well spent. Are you hungry?"

It wasn't until then that Reign realized she'd barely eaten anything at Alexa's dinner party, and the vision had taken so much out of her. She tried to remain nonchalant regarding her revelation, but was given away with a sudden, and very unladylike, rumbling of her stomach.

"Maybe a little," she conceded.

Dominic helped her up off of the bed and they walked into the living room. No matter how much strength he had just seen in her, or how well put together she tried so make herself appear, he could tell she was exhausted. How much could one person endure without showing signs of the toll taken on them?

"Ok, so why don't you sit down and relax and I'll see what you have in the kitchen."

Reign stopped just short of sitting on the sofa. "How about I change and get comfortable while you do that. I'm thinking the need for formal wear has passed."

The way Dominic looked at her told Reign that he did not want to let her out of his sight, and she really couldn't blame him. Her little *incident* probably terrified him.

"I'll be fine. I'm just going to change and I'll be right back out. Promise," she added with a smile.

Reign could tell he was still hesitant when she turned to head back into the bedroom, but she had to get out of her clothes. Once in her room, she closed the door and leaned against it. Nothing had drained her as much as that last vision had; and she wasn't completely sure, but it was probably due to using her powers. Although the fact that she could use them while in a vision was something she was unaware of until that moment.

After taking a few deep breaths, Reign made her way to the closet and pulled out one of her many pairs of sweat pants and a t-shirt. She wasn't interested in the least at looking cute; all she wanted was to be able to move freely without the fear of something popping out.

Upon emerging from the bedroom, Reign smiled at seeing Dominic standing in front of the stove, diligently chopping and stirring. He really looked at home in the kitchen.

"I poured some orange juice for you. It's here on the island," he said without turning around.

Reign walked toward the kitchen, still looking at him. He was intently focused on the culinary mission at hand. "And can I ask what masterpiece you're attempting to create in my kitchen?"

"You *can* ask, but that doesn't mean I'm going to tell you," he answered with a slight smile. "Besides, I'm considering taking that word *attempting* as mild disrespect, and the worse thing a hungry customer can do is insult the chef."

Sitting at the island Reign was happy with their easy comradery, along with the fact that Dominic wasn't drilling her with fifty questions.

"You forget sir, Grace adores me. All I have to do is tell her that you withheld food at a time that I was in questionable health and she very well may never cook for you again."

He abruptly stopped chopping whatever was in front of him as if in thought, then turned to face her. "You drive a hard bargain Madame," he said with a straight face, then turned back to the cutting board.

A half hour later, Reign and Dominic were sitting at her dining room table eating a creamy pasta and seafood dish that she was falling more and more in love with after every bite.

"When I was at Eden didn't you say something about not being able to cook?" Reign asked accusingly.

"Cooking is not my forte; however, I do have a few specialties that Grace taught me."

"Well, hats off to her for saving my life tonight," she laughed in response.

Dominic gave her a few inconspicuous glances as he continued to eat. He found it odd that she was more attractive to him now, underdressed and make-up free, than he did when she was all put together. Reign seemed much more at peace and in her element right now. The only thing that felt wrong was her thick curly hair that was still straight and fine from her visit to the salon earlier that day.

After they'd finished eating and loaded the dishwasher, Dominic checked the time and saw it was after midnight. "I really didn't intend on being here this late, I apologize."

"No, it's perfectly fine. Besides, if you weren't here I probably *would* be lying down, but I'd be starving. I had no energy for anything earlier. I barely had the strength to change my clothes, let alone cook."

"I want you to know how serious I was though," he said while putting his shoes back on from when he'd removed them earlier. "I will be checking on you quite a bit. I don't know if this is an option for you, but maybe you'd want to put me in touch with some of your emergency contacts. I don't want to leave anything to chance."

As he got up, Reign admitted to herself that she was a little upset that he had to go. "Yeah, I'll consider that. I really want to tell you not to worry, but I'm sure you're set on being my personal hero, so I won't offend your efforts."

Walking to the door was slightly awkward, especially for Reign. Her attraction to him was more than a little intense, but so were her feelings for Krystian. She couldn't choose one without feeling the emptiness of losing the other. So, if she were to kiss Dominic as her impulsive side was begging her to do, Reign knew she'd have to let go of any expectation of a romantic reconciliation with Krystian.

"Well, I hope to see you soon...when I'm not protectively stalking you that is," Dominic said with a brilliant smile once they'd reached the door.

Reign tiptoed up and kissed him on the cheek, "I'd like that. And thank you for everything."

He stared at her for a moment, then gently caressed her cheek with his hand. For a split second Reign felt his aura change to a mustard yellow and saw a flicker of pain in his eyes. Something was wrong but she didn't know what.

"Until next time my princess," were his last words to her before he was out the door and walking into the desolate night air.

Reign didn't know it, but her entire evening had been played out for peeping eyes, like a star-crossed romance scene. The prying intruder hadn't been privy to her home life as of late since she had begun closing her curtains after sunset, so this was a treat.

"Made a new friend I see," he said with a smirk that more accurately resembled a sneer.

Donovan had arrived only days ago but was already cutting into what precious little time he had to indulge in Ms. La'Roche. She had her hooks in him and didn't even know it.

He was pulled from his thoughts by the ringing of his phone. "Yes?"

"Donovan wants to meet tomorrow night," a voice said from the other end.

"Okay. Text me the time and location," he replied, then disconnected the phone.

He was getting tired of the demands and having to do everything on Donovan's terms. But there was no way around it; Reign was consuming his every thought. If he were to have any chance at quelling his mounting urges, Donovan had to be appeased.

Looking from his balcony back toward where her house sat nestled between a small sycamore and a fringe tree, he could see that she'd closed her curtains. He wondered what she was doing now. Was she lathering her golden hued skin with the lavender scented soap that he'd caught a whiff of many times in passing; or was she snuggled deep down in the queen-sized bed where her blood had once spilled.

Thinking about that night left him wanting. No matter how many times he replayed it he could not figure out how she'd lived through the extremely precise incisions from his knife. It didn't matter though, because the next time she met his blade, he'd make sure that the resulting outcome was permanent. He'd make sure that the last face that those enticing amber eyes would ever be set upon was his.

Chapter 14

When Reign closed her eyes, Dominic was still in the forefront of her mind. There was also the catastrophe of a run-in with Krystian earlier. She'd never felt so hopelessly confused and consumed by two men so completely in her life, and she had no clue what to do about it. So instead of continuing to think on it, she decided to seek refuge in her sleep.

The instant Reign closed her eyes she was dreaming. However, this was unlike any dream she'd had in the past. Looking out, she found herself standing in the middle of an open field and the sun beat down warmly against her face. In that moment she allowed herself a second to indulge, even though she knew it was not real.

Overcome with the peacefulness of her surroundings she stood there, looking off into the distance. There was something so calming about where she was that it almost felt wrong. *It's too perfect,* she thought to herself, and began walking aimlessly through the flower speckled field.

It felt like she had been wandering for some time when Reign spotted someone walking toward her. Whoever it was appeared to be just as serene and inviting as the field she'd been meandering through, but she couldn't help it when her wariness rose. Reign didn't recognize the person but could tell it was a woman, and there was an odd sense of familiarity about her.

About the same height as her, the woman had a chestnut complexion and a pile of thick curly hair sat atop her head. But there was something else, something intensely recognizable about the woman that had Reign staring so intently. Then, when she was only a few feet away, she finally figured out what it was...her eyes. They were so clear that her irises almost looked nonexistent .

"Nimekuwa kusubiri kwa muda mrefu kukutana na wewe," the woman said when she approached Reign.

"I'm sorry, I don't understand your language."

"My language," she replied incredulously with her thick accent. "Did they teach you nothing?"

Reign was confused. The woman seemed quite harmless, but was being very condescending. "I assure you, just because I don't know the language you were speaking does not mean my intellect should be open for discussion or questioned."

"So you do not know who I am?"

They stood there staring at one another, and while her mind was screaming that she *should* know who this woman was, Reign continued to draw a blank. "No, I don't. But I do feel a strong connection."

The woman smiled and took Reign's hand as she sat in the grass. "Sitting would probably be best for this talk."

Taking a seat next to her, Reign was almost prepared for the worst, but changed her mind. None of her other dreams or visions ever allowed her this much solace. Not to mention there was none of the sulfur or intense morbidity of Nicola's mind games.

"I am Tempest," she said, breaking the momentary silence.

"But, you can't be...."

"I assure you I am," Tempest said, cutting Reign off. "I am here because your mother and grandmother's spirits called to and woke me. They said you needed help and advised me of Nicola's interferences."

"But why would they reach out to you?"

Tempest smiled briefly, aware of the toll her twin sister and father's antics took on their name. "My sister and I may be twins, but we are nothing alike. I've come to accept that I am the light and she is the dark of the same coin."

"What gave it away?" Reign asked with more sarcasm than she had intended.

The upset was evident in Tempest's eyes. She did love her sister; how could she be expected not to. But she couldn't let her destroy their family.

"I know you think me crazy for still caring about her, but we are more than sisters. For so long Nicola was the part of me that could never be complete. My empathy, love, devotion to helping others made me vulnerable to the things of existence. And until my rebirth in death, she filled that void."

Reign thought about what Tempest had just said, and though she didn't have a sibling, she did have Alexa. "I get it…kind of. But she's still batshit crazy."

"There is something you need to know," Tempest began again with a heavy sigh, ignoring Reign's supposition of her sister. "The only way for you to truly understand the web of your family, and Nicola to an extent, is to see it."

Tempest positioned herself so that she was now facing Reign, then held her hands out, palms up.

Reign looked at her hesitantly. She wanted to trust this woman who was her great aunt, but she'd left too much to chance recently and it had cost her a great deal.

Sensing her apprehension, Tempest sighed, "I know your concerns, but think about it. If I wanted to bring harm to you, I could have done it before you even knew who I was. I am here to help. I am here to clean up a mess that my sister and father made nearly a century ago."

Once again, Tempest held out her hands. Only after a brief second Reign followed suit, allowing her palms to rest in her aunt's.

"Reign, you have a few natural gifts: premonition, supernatural sight, and walking into the past. You don't see what *has* happened simply because you are a legacy. You do so because that is a portion of what is in you that allows people, and beings, to communicate with you."

"Like when granmé Sophie and pépé Hania came to me?"

"Yes. That could not have been done if you did not first have the gift beloved. This is one of the many reasons you are so special. Your natural abilities are comprised of generations of individuals that have had one, *maybe* two, of your many gifts."

It was as though the universe was continuously on a secret mission to convince Reign that she was this *chosen* person everyone kept saying she was. From learning to fight to everything aligning to help her with the awakening of her gifts. None of it could be coincidence, could it?

"I am going to open my mind to you," Tempest continued. "In order for you to become your predestined self, there's a dormant part of your mind that needs to be stirred. Just breathe, relax and let your sight guide the way."

Reign took a deep breath as Tempest's hands closed around hers. She allowed her mind to calm, and when she could feel her aunt's energy, she let go completely.

New Orleans, Louisiana- January 2, 1931

"But it doesn't make any sense," Nicola said with much frustration. "I have never had a premonition in my life. That is Tempest's gift, not mine."

Nicola was aggravated over a dream she'd had the night before. The number ten was symbolized everywhere, and she held a baby that she'd somehow known would never be hers.

C.J. wanted to tell his daughter of the forbidden magick he was practicing, but he knew Nicola wouldn't be completely on board with his decision just yet. The only way for her to reach the full potential of their bloodline was for her to syphon Tempest's legacy *and* natural gifts. And although he had begun the process, breaking a hoodoo magick law such as this would require a great sacrifice; one that Nicola had to be ready to accept when the time came.

"Nothing we do would ever make sense to the *quelconque*. They have simple minds that we are above, so you have to stop thinking like one of them."

"Pær, must you look down on everyone that is not us?"

C.J. walked over to where his daughter sat on the living room sofa. It was like she couldn't see the big picture of all they did and it was frustrating him. Too much of his wife was in his daughters, but Nicola was the stronger of the two. He could not let her doubt and affections jeopardize everything he'd work so hard to build.

"Because they are not us. And until you see that, you may as well be one of them," and with those words he turned and headed out the front door.

Nicola sat there, wishing she could feel some other emotion besides hurt. Only three people in this life had ever mattered enough to cause her pain, and one was already dead.

Looking around, she felt pride in how far they'd come since her mother had died. From a questionable home in the marshland surrounded by swamp water, to living a life of luxury in the thriving metropolis that was New Orleans. And it was all because of her father.

"Is he gone?" Tempest asked, descending the stairs.

"Yes. But I still don't understand why you feel the need to continuously avoid him Temp. You act like he's out for your blood?"

"Sometimes it feels that way," she said softly, walking over to and sitting by her sister. "You wouldn't feel that way because you are the strong one...his golden child."

Nicola looked at her sister. Tempest was beautiful, with her deep rich skin, sun streaked midnight hair and crystalline eyes. But over the last couple of years she'd become so fragile, emotionally and physically. Nicola could see that Tempest continued to grieve for their mother, even though she was able to call on her spirit any time she wanted. And maybe that was the reason she couldn't let go.

"Temp, I need you to stop calling on mama. The only way for you to get better is to free yourself of her."

Looking at Nicola with pained eyes, Tempest could tell her sister that that was impossible, but she'd never be able to tell her why. When she was alive, Aiyana had the gift of premonition. Since her death, she'd come to Tempest in her dreams and warn her of what was to come. At first, she thought that missing her mother was what caused the dreams; but as time progressed, so did the urgency of her dreams. Aiyana had warned Tempest that she'd take her last breath at the hands of her father from a choice made by her sister.

Looking into Nicola's almost purple eyes, Tempest had to believe that she'd make the right choice. That she wouldn't willfully bring harm to her only sister and twin.

"Nic, do you hate me?" she asked.

"How could you ask me that?" Nicola responded, genuinely appalled.

"I don't know. Sometimes it feels like you're in another place. And the way you look at me, like you're considering something...*bad*."

Nicola rose from the couch and began to slowly pace back and forth. It was true that since their father told her she was the strong one, and that one day Tempest's powers would be her own, she'd tried to figure out what life would be like without her twin. But that didn't mean she'd intentionally cause her harm. How could she exist without the only person that knew her better than she knew herself?

"I love you. No matter what happens in this life I need you to know that," Nicola finally said, then turned to look at Tempest. "There is no one on this earth that is closer to me, or that I love more, than you."

Though they were probably meant to be endearing words, there was a foreboding undertone that Tempest could not shake. Her mother was right, her life was in Nicola's hands. Over the past few weeks, her premonitions had become slightly hazy and she was only able to make out bits and pieces of her visions. She had to spell her gift to see anything with certainty, but it was draining. There was something deep within her that told Tempest that she should invoke a vision spell, and soon.

New Orleans, Louisiana- January 31, 1931

Over the past couple of weeks Nicola had fought the ultimatums that her father had presented, and it was wearing her down. C.J. finally confided in her that Tempest's life would not and could not pass on through natures calling; her days had to be ended at her sister's own hand. This was the only way for Nicola to obtain both natural and legacy magicks from Tempest.

"You cannot expect me to kill my sister," Nicola had said frantically.

"Your sister will not live much longer," he lied, "you'd be doing her a favor while also taking an opportunity to be something mighty."

Nicola paused and looked at her father, "Temp is dying?"

"Mon amour, look at your sister. *Really* look at her. She's thin and frail, and I fear will go out of her mind with grief soon. What quality of life is she to have?"

"But…I can't," she replied weakly.

C.J. took his daughter's hand and sat her down on the sitting room sofa.

"There is something that I have not told you," he began, briefly cupping her cheek. "The dream you've been having, it's a warning. I can't say for sure what the warning is, and you won't be able to either until you can see it. What I can tell you though is that you have ten years to figure it out. That's why it's so repetitive in the dream. You have to find out what the ancestors are trying to tell you before it's too late."

For the remainder of the day, Nicola took every opportunity to truly see her sister. She watched Tempest, and for the first time saw how much she'd changed since losing their mother. Her grief was constant and she barely ate. How had she survived for so long living like this? Her father was right; she existed only because she could not die.

As Nicola sat anxiously looking at the clock while awaiting her father's arrival, she thought about the insight he provided regarding the dreams she'd been having since the New Year. He'd told her that the dreams signified the birth of one meant to bring about her demise; he said it was a warning. But she couldn't see any of them clearly, and would not until they'd performed the ritual and she had Tempest's powers.

Early that evening C.J. had brought her into the cellar of their townhouse that he'd always kept locked. There was a black robe, several lit candles, spices and herbs hanging from the ceiling, and a sacrificial altar that sat in the middle of the room. He told her to change, then left.

Nicola sat there for what felt like hours, waiting in dread for the unknown that her father would bring. As she sat there patiently, trying to focus her mind and energy, she caught something in the corner of her eye. A shadow, but shaped like a woman, sat hidden in a dark corner of the cellar; and the more Nicola focused on it, the clearer it became.

"Mère," she said with tears in her eyes.

For years since her mother passed Nicola tried to call on her, but Aiyana would never come. Finally she came to terms with the fact that she just wasn't as powerful as Tempest in that regard, and gave up trying.

Aiyana emerged from out of the shadows and seemed to glide toward her. She looked just as Nicola remembered. A deep and impossibly smooth ebony skin tone, eyes the color of cocoa, strong African features that were a testament to her bloodline, and a mass of thick kinky hair that she often kept in a poof atop her head.

Nicola stood there, frozen, as her mother made her way to her. She couldn't believe that after all of the tears and attempts to reach out, Aiyana was finally revealing herself.

"Upendo wangu, unafanya nini?" Aiyana said in her native tongue.

"Mother, I haven't spoken Swahili since you left us."

"I know child," Aiyana replied, "I've been watching you. I said, 'my love, what are you doing?'"

"I am taking my rightful place, and sparing Tempest years of pain and hardship in the process," Nicola replied, looking up at her mother.

Aiyana closed her eyes for a moment, then focused back on Nicola. "Your father lies to you my child. What he wants for you is absolute power, and the only way for that to happen is by killing Tempest."

"No, he would not lie to me!" she shouted and stood up to face her mother.

"He *would* lie to you. Eventually, I grew to love your father, but he is a manipulative man. By ensuring your place as the *celebrant*, he solidifies his favor with the shetani, and his return to this life."

"No, you lie. He is good, and loves me! He would never trade his light for such evil. And why is it you only come to me now after years of comforting Tempest!?"

Nicola was angry, and was becoming angrier by the second. No longer looking at her mother, she walked up to the altar and slammed her clenched fists into it. She couldn't believe that her mother was coming not to console her, but to beg for Tempest's life.

"Daughter please, what you are doing is wrong and uncalled for. You have power and greatness of your own...you are of Chidike blood. Don't taint yourself this way by taking your sister's life."

Nicola could feel her energy increasing and with the full force of her mother's tongue, she commanded Aiyana's spirit away, never to return to her.

"Nenda na kamwe kurudi!"

Then she sat waiting, once again, for her father's return.

When Tempest woke, she found herself lying on an altar of cold grey stone, with her sister and father standing on either side of her. The room they were in was dark with only the flicker of several candles bouncing off of the walls.

"What is going on, and why can't I move?" she asked.

"We are going to put your mind and body at ease my dear sister. No one loves you more than me, and for this reason, I must be the one to silence your life."

"No Nic, you don't have to do this," Tempests words were pleading, but she was calm. If this was how her life was to end, she would not spend her final few moments afraid.

"I know...but I want to," she replied.

It was then that Tempest saw an almost sadistic look in her sister's eyes. She recognized Nicola's face but her aura was a dark grey, tar-like and unrecognizable. Then she turned her head to look at her father, who stood there quietly with a smirk, as if awaiting some grand prize. He almost looked inhuman, and his aura was not just dark, it was rancid.

Then, without any warning, Nicola lashed out with the blade in her hand and sliced her father's throat. Blood flowed from his neck, covering Tempest. She screamed in shock, but only for a second. When C.J. had finally collapsed dead to the stone floor, Tempest looked up and directly into the eyes of her mother.

"Everything will be fine," she said, gently caressing her daughter's forehead. This will all be over soon, and your spirit will join mine in love and peace."

"I'm ready," were Tempest's final words before Nicola's blade drew multiple precise incisions in her skin, allowing her blood to flow freely.

When Tempest spoke her last words, Nicola thought that they were being declared in surrender. But because she'd expelled Aiyana, she couldn't see the final precious moment shared by her sister and mother. So, thinking that she'd just triumphed, Nicola began carving Latin sigils into her sister's hands as instructed by her father.

"Quod autem nunc mea eius. Et auferam sanguinem legatum soluere machinam," she began chanting over and over until the flames from the candles were extinguished. Then, as Nicola stood there cloaked in darkness, one by one the candles ignited once more, but with the flicker of a blood red glow.

A feeling overcame her that she couldn't describe even if she were to try. Her body radiated in heat as she collapsed to the floor, overcome with a wave of sensations. Then she smiled, because she knew it had worked. All of Tempest powers were fleeing her lifeless corpse and taking residence in their new host.

Then, when Nicola felt that she was finally in control, she pushed herself up off of the floor. She hadn't realized it before, but she'd become covered in her father and sister's blood. Then she looked as each of them. Her father was a fallen heap on the stone floor, but there was something different about Tempest. She wasn't of the same frail form that she'd grown use to over the past few years. Yes, she was lifeless, but her body was full and well formed. She didn't look sickly at all.

Then it hit her. C.J. had spelled her all these years, making her see what he had wanted. There was nothing wrong with Tempest, and she doubted she would have died anytime soon. But oddly enough, Nicola felt no remorse. She was actually glad that her father had taken matters into his own hands. Her full potential could have never been reached with Tempest still moping about; and now she was free of her, and free to do as she pleased. She was an all-powerful Priestess.

Then, as Nicola descended the steps of the alter and headed to the doorway, she was struck with an intensity that almost knocked her to the ground. She was having a vision, but not just any vision. She was seeing the dream that she'd been having for the past thirty days.

Focusing, Nicola's surroundings changed and became the setting of her dream. She was in the bedroom of a house and there were people hurrying about.

"Hot water, get me more hot water," a man's voice demanded.

"Push! You can't give up now, keep pushing," she heard a woman say.

"Almost there," the man's voice came again. "Almost there. One more push should do it."

Then there was a shrill wail of a baby. Nicola turned and began walking toward the direction of the cries.

"Ennelise, it's a girl," the woman said, just as Nicola entered the room. "What will you call her?"

The woman was lying in the bed, sweat dripping from her brow. And despite having just given birth to a tiny human, she smiled brightly. Then the woman called Ennelise looked up to a man that was standing protectively over mother and child and nodded, smiling up at him.

"Sophie. Her name is Sophie."

As she began to focus her attention on the baby, Nicola saw something strange. There was a crude drawing of a snake and a big black dot on her forehead. That had to mean something, but she had no clue what. Then, the room went black, and she was back in her dimly lit cellar.

"Sophie," she said aloud. "What exactly is the reason for you disrupting my life, and more importantly, where are you?"

When Reign opened her eyes and looked up at Tempest they were filled with tears.

"You were both wronged and deceived. How could your father be so manipulative?"

Tempest looked at her great niece, and her empathy touched her. "My dear, Nicola had a choice, and made a choice. Our father could only blind her but so much and for so long before she had to see the truth. Deep down, it's what she wanted."

Taking a deep breath, Reign used her hand and wiped her tear stained face. "And Grandma Sophie? What does she have to do with any of this?"

Knowing her next words would be the most difficult to hear, Tempest averted her eyes for just a moment before continuing.

"Nicola saw Sophie because she was the one to give birth to the child that would cause her legacy heir to rebel in love. An intertwining with the Etienne bloodline was foretold to bring forth the child to end her rule. *You* are that child."

Reign sat in deep thought for a moment. Things still weren't making sense to her, especially since she *was* born. "I think I'm more confused now than ever."

"Eventually Nicola figured out that the symbols on Sophie's head were Native American. They referenced rebellion and death. The problem that Nicola ran into was that she didn't know the origin of those symbols, and by the time she figured it out, Sophie had already been born. So, she did what she thought was the next best thing by killing your grandfather; but yet again, she was too late.

By then Claudette had been born. And when your parents met, she was bent on keeping the two of them separate, and so, cursed any offspring they may have had. She did call for your mother's blood, but Claudette's legacy is quite strong as well, and her life force did not succumb to Nicola's magick until you were of age."

It was a lot to take in all at once. Her great grandmother tried to kill her grandmother, and when that failed, killed her grandfather to keep her mother from being born.

"That's why the purple light glowed around my grandfather as his body burned on the pyre."

"Yes," Tempest answered. "It was a silencing and enslavement spell. She didn't want to take a chance of him revealing certain truths to you. And since Sophie never knew, she was not of concern."

"But..." Reign began, "she's dead. What kind of powers or influence could she possibly have as a corpse?"

"When she stole my gifted and legacy magic, it elevated her to a new type of creature. She broke Voodoo law; as a result she became an unnatural being and is grasping for immortality. Since you are the key to her final death, you are also the key to that immortality. If you lose, she can incinerate your soul and take full possession of your body...and your magick."

"Incinerate, as in..."

"As in you will cease to exist on any plane. But dawn is breaking, and I must leave you now. I promise I will not be too far. If you ever need me, just call; and remember, always trust your gifts."

And with that, Tempest was gone. Reign was left alone in the beautiful and impossibly green field to mull over everything she'd just learned. *How* was any of this even possible? Just when she thought her problems only consisted of two ridiculously handsome men and an annoying ghost, fate gave her another hard and swift kick in the ass.

Chapter 15

When Reign woke the sun was already high in the sky and stained glass mosaics of her French doors were casting an array of colors around the room. But unfortunately, she was not in a mindset to soak up the beauty surrounding her.

She laid there thinking about everything she'd just learned and how as her world was piecing together, it was also falling apart. Reign was content to lay there for a bit when she heard a knock at the door.

"Just a sec," she yelled, grabbing her sweatpants off the floor, hopping into them and heading to the door.

Looking through the sidelight, she could see it was her father.

"What are you doing here," Reign asked, opening the door to let him in.

Julien did not speak until he was fully in the house and she'd closed the door.

"Did you have a vision last night?" he asked.

Reign knew that he didn't know all the details and just how far his grandmother was willing to go to make, and keep, her presence iron clad. And knowing how deeply his love for her mother ran, to finally have confirmation that his grandmother was the reason she died would truly hurt him.

"Sit down, then we can talk."

He wanted to put up a fight and demand that his daughter stop coddling him, but he knew it would be pointless. She'd lost so much, and she was desperately trying to protect what little she had left, so he conceded and sat on the sofa.

"Now, tell me what you know," Julien said.

Reign put on some water for tea then sat next to him before speaking. "I will, but first, how did you know about the vision?"

"Your mother, she's been coming to me a lot lately. She said that your aunt Tempest would pay you a visit."

Well, now she had no choice. Her father obviously knew way too much for her to tiptoe around the truth. So she told him everything, from C.J.'s manipulation of Nicola, to her attempt at murdering Sophie and success in taking Tempest and Claudette's lives. And just as she'd predicted, the pain that shown on his face was unbearable.

"The water is boiling. I'm going to make you some tea," she coaxed, getting up and heading to the kitchen.

She couldn't bear seeing her father in such agony. And she didn't doubt that with the revelation, he felt guilty for at least Claudette's murder. Logic said that all of it was completely out of his control, but love has a terrible way of playing games of guilt on the mind.

"You know how much I love you, right?" she asked Julien, handing him a cup of piping hot lavender tea.

"Of course I do mon amour."

"Were it not for you and maman, I would not be here. Only the two of you could have brought me into this would, and I know for a fact she doesn't regret a moment of the love you shared. Please, take the burden of the action of others off your shoulders," she said, placing her hand on his arm for emphasis. "For a moment I felt so sorry for Nicola, but Tempest said something that made me think. She said that, even though she was deceived by her father, Nicola eventually saw the truth…and she made a choice. Papa, don't take the blame for *her* choice."

"How did Iwa ever bless me with such a daughter? You make me proud. I know your light will shine brightly as the sun."

Julien stood up and drank the last sip of his tea, then began walking to the door. He was so strong and proud, and Reign was sure that he could withstand anything that would come his way.

"You're sure you don't want to stay a little longer?"

"No child, I have many things to do," but he stopped just before walking out the door. "You must ward this house, and do it soon. Nicola grows stronger with each passing day, and she *will* come for you. Don't make it easy for her. And spell any weapons you may have."

"Je t'aime tant de père," she said with a grin.

"Your French is improving," Julien replied with a big smile. "And I love you too."

Once her father left, Reign brushed her teeth, then headed to the kitchen to make breakfast. Since Julien's visit had had forced her out of bed, she hadn't gotten a chance to process everything she'd learned. But the hardest part of the revelation was the fact that Nicola had killed her grandfather, which left her grandmother heartbroken and alone. Then she thought about what her father had said to her about warding the house. He was definitely right about that. Reign's strength may have been increasing, but she was nowhere near ready to take on the likes of her great grandmother.

After making her food, Reign sat at the dining room table and ate in the early morning silence. She had so many questions, but didn't know where the answers were going to come from. And that wasn't even the worst of her problems; she was running out of time.

Just as she finished eating and was about to get up, Reign's phone rang.

"Hello?"

"Hey Reign. Do you have a second to talk?" Alexa asked from the other end.

"Yeah. I just finished eating. About to get dressed for church," Reign answered.

"How do you do it?"

"Do what?"

Alexa paused for a moment, as if considering her question. "With all that's going on, all of the things that you know for a fact that exist, how can you still manage to have faith that there is something greater than all of it?"

"I don't know," Reign began. "I guess that's the reason I can believe. Knowing that there is a supernatural force, things that people are so frightened by that they shove them into horror movies, this greater presence *has* to exist to balance it…right?"

"Reign, you have to stop doubting yourself and your abilities. None of this was by chance, you were chosen for a reason. Your faith is a weapon in itself."

Getting up from the table with plate in hand, Reign went to dump everything into the sink. Then she headed to the bathroom and started going through her clothes for church service.

"Ok Lex, I know you didn't just call to get all sappy and tell me you believe in me."

"Oh yeah. I wanted to give you a heads up."

"What for?"

"I just overheard Adrian and Krys talking. He's coming over to see you later. Something about the dinner party and his brother. He really wants to talk to you."

"I'm sure he does," Reign muttered. It would be so much easier for them both if he just let her go. She was getting tired of the back and forth and apparent obstacles by every force imaginable insistent on keeping them apart.

"Look, I can't talk much longer, but I wanted to let you know."

"Ok thanks. I'm about to start getting dressed so I can get out of here, but I'll call you later and let you know what happens."

And the universe keeps dishing it out, Reign thought to herself after hanging up the phone. It was apparent that she wasn't going to get any of the peace she so desperately craved anytime soon. If it wasn't Nicola it was her father, if it wasn't Dominic it was Krystian...and now Tempest was communicating with her and sharing information that could potentially change it all.

Reign opted for a searing hot shower, but even that didn't clear her mind. There was sage scented everything from the gift set Dominic sent to her, and every time she caught a whiff of it, thoughts of him flooded her senses so completely it was almost unbearable.

Frustrated with everything, she decided to go to noon church service and on her way back, pick up everything she'd need to complete the warding spell. It would be the first time she'd ever performed any type of magick willfully, and would likely assess her current strength. Within the hour Reign was out the door, eager to have what little solace she was able to get.

It was about three thirty when Reign returned home. Being out in the fresh air and hearing an empowering word from Pastor Spencer was just what she needed to balance herself. After service she'd made a few stops at local shops that carried the kinds of *specialty* items she'd need to complete the warding ritual.

After changing, Reign removed four red candles from her bag and placed one at every entry point of the house. Then, once the curtains were closed, she positioned herself in the center of the living room and placed the herbs she's purchased on a piece of white linen.

Bay leaves, elderberries, salt and coal were laid out before her. Taking a deep breath, she began to chant while grinding the coal and salt in a small wooden bowl.

"Spiritibus exaudi me. Custodi ex utraque parte ostiorum, Hanc domum praesidio numquam separari permittas. Spiritibus exaudi me. Custodi ex utraque parte ostiorum. Hanc domum praesidio numquam separari permittas.

As she continued to chant and grind the salt and coal mixture into a fine powder, the hairs on the back of her neck began to stand, like someone was in the room with her. Then, looking up and directly across from her, she spoke.

"Reveal yourself to me."

Reign was not surprised when, just as quickly as she declared the words, Tempest appeared before her.

"What are you doing?" Reign asked, irritated by her aunt's timing.

"You are growing much stronger. To not only sense, but to call on me like that…yes, you will be ready soon."

"I've always been able to sense spirits. That was no big deal."

"It is a big deal Reign. In the past, you could feel some spirits, only those that allowed you to. But I'm sure you could never command one to reveal themselves before."

Reign did not want to admit it, but the things Tempest was implying frightened her. She was not ready to even be *almost* ready.

"It's *not* a big deal," she emphasized again.

"Niece, this is coming for you whether you want it to or not. So, for all of our sakes, don't hinder the progress you've made simply because you are afraid."

Then Tempest picked up the bowl that the elderberries and been placed in and began crushing them.

"And why is it that you speak Latin and not Creole when you chant?"

Reign was becoming frustrated. All she wanted to do was spell the protection barrier and be lazy for two seconds before Krystian showed up. But as life would have it, she'd get no peace for a while.

"Because spirits communicate with ancient languages, and hoodoo magick becomes fouled when spoken in a *quelconque* tongue. I don't know how to spell in the old Creole language, but Latin just comes to me."

Tempest ceased grinding the elderberries and looked up at Reign. "All that you've said is true and makes perfect sense. But did you know that if you spoke in the original Voodoun language of our ancestors, Swahili, your gris-gris could be ten times stronger?"

"But I was never taught that tongue."

"You don't have to be taught the tongue Reign. It's a part of you, just as is Creole. All you have to do it *remember* it."

Very intrigued by what she was being told, Reign agreed to allow Tempest to guide her.

"The bay leaves must burn right?"

Reign nodded her head in agreement.

"Now, which do you think would command the greatest notice of the spirits? Lighting it with a match, or holding it in your hand and calling down the flames *Princesse*?"

Looking at Tempest for only a moment, Reign picked up the bowl of bay leaves then dumped them in her hands. She sat there, cupping the leaves as her aunt guided her.

"Now close your eyes and pay attention. You are the physical manifestation of two great bloodlines, the spirits will speak to you…you just have to listen. Ask them for the words of the great ones before you."

Reign closed her eyes as instructed and focused intently on everything unseen around her.   Her breathing was controlled and after a while, she began to hear the whispers of a multitude of voices. It was like standing in the center of a crowded room, unable to hear just one person.

"You control them, they do not control you. Single out the answer to the question you seek; hear only what matters," Tempest directed.

Then the voices separated and she was able to make out one repetitive phrase: *Lazima kulinda nyumba hii. Hakuna uovu anaweza kuingia milango hizi.*

"I can hear the answer," Reign said, her eyes still closed.

"Now, remember what I said, you are the physical manifestation of two great bloodlines. Begin in utterance with the words of your mother and channel that energy; then, finish with the language of your father."

"*Spiritibus exaudi me. Custodi ex utraque parte ostiorum, Hanc domum praesidio numquam separari permittas.*" Then Reign paused for a brief moment before continuing, "*Lazima kulinda nyumba hii. Hakuna uovu anaweza kuingia milango hizi.*"

Intently chanting the words over and over, she didn't notice that the leaves in her hand had grown warm.

"Now speak to them both. Tell them what you want and they will be as one in your command!" Tempest implored.

"*Ignis Kuwasha!*"

No sooner had she said it did the leaves ignite and burned brightly. Reign opened her eyes, in complete awe of what she'd just done. In the palm of her hands, a flame burned intensely, but was only warm to the touch, and did not singe her hands.

"Look," Tempest said, pointing to the candles that she'd placed by the kitchen doorway earlier.

The wick was burning intensely. Then Reign turned toward the bedroom and she could see the flicker of flame from the candle by the French doors. Then, she looked back at her palms where the leaves burned unceasingly until the flames had consumed them completely.

Tempest continued to look at Reign as she sat there in awe, "Now you must finish it."

Standing, Reign picked up the two bowls with the salt coal mixture and crushed elderberries, placing a small portion of each at every door and window. When she was finally done and seated on the sofa, she remained silent for a moment.

"I really am this *one* that everyone keeps talking about, aren't I?" Reign said decisively.

"What gave it away, mpenzi wangu?"

"My love...mpenzi wangu means my love. How can I possibly know that?" Reign questioned almost desperately.

"Be open to what the spirits are saying to you. Your knowledge is in your blood, not your mind. When you spoke Latin, was it something you were taught, or did you just know it?"

Reign had never even thought of that. And if she were to be honest with herself, aside from her meditative guidance, everything else she did came naturally. Even the warding spell, she just kind of *knew* what to do.

"No, I wasn't taught Latin," she reiterated.

"These two remarkably different cultures had to merge for you to exist. Both great on their own but mighty together, and humbled by your faith and perspective that there *is* one greater. Whereas Nicola believes she was the greatest until you; and will be the greatest once again after she takes you. She wants forever...immortality. So see, whether you succeed or fail, you are the key."

"When you say it, it seems so intense. But I don't feel shaken or unsure anymore. So much life has been stolen at her hand, and it has to end."

Tempest smiled, "Now you are allowing yourself to grow."

Then Reign was in her living room, with only the glow of candlelight, alone. Left to sort out all her thoughts, unanswered question, and newfound strength. She felt like maybe life wasn't just shoveling crap her way. That there was a purpose for all of this and she was finally figuring it out. Then the doorbell rang.

Chapter 16

It was nearing dusk when Krystian rang Reign's doorbell. The way things were left the other day was not as how he had hoped. When Adrian told him that she was going to be there, he was on edge for days leading up to the dinner party. Since she was finally cordial to him he figured that maybe, just maybe, there'd be a chance for them to get back to where they once were. Well, that was until his brother showed up.

Nathan and Krystian had never been particularly close, even for twins. For some odd reason, Donovan took to his younger son and fought tooth and nail with the eldest. Ever since they were old enough to understand their father's business, Nathan was all about appeasing him, while Krystian wanted nothing more than to see it all come crumbling down. So naturally, when his twin brother came knocking on his door at three in the morning, Krystian was skeptical.

He didn't know what he'd accomplish by talking to Reign. Actually, Alexa had tried her hardest to talk him out of it.

"Wouldn't it make more sense to call her? Maybe even *ask* to come over as opposed to just showing up. What if she has company?"

He'd thought of all of that, but seeing her again changed something in him. Being around her was like sitting in an electrically charged room just waiting for lightening to strike.

Then the door opened.

"Hi. What are you doing here?" Reign said calmly. To his surprise she didn't look the least bit upset about him being there.

"I was wondering if we could talk for a second?" Krystian asked, hoping he didn't sound like he was begging.

Reign opened the door to let him in. "Yeah, sure. I have a little free time."

When Krystian walked in, only the illuminated glow of the candles filled the room. If he hadn't known what was going on in her life, he would have wrongly assumed that she was attempting to set a mood. But he *did* know better.

"Meditating?" he asked.

"No," Reign replied, walking back from the kitchen with two glasses in hand. "Actually, my aunt was guiding me with a spell and teaching me how to strengthen my gifts."

"Oh, I didn't mean to interrupt. Where is she? I can leave," Krystian said, about to get up from the sofa.

Reign put up her hand to stop him. "It's not like that. You *do* remember I have…gifts, right?"

"You mean like the super strength and seeing dead people?"

She laughed before continuing. "Yes, exactly. Well as it turns out, I can do a lot more. My aunt Tempest, Nicola's twin sister, came to me and revealed so much. She's been guiding and helping me."

No matter how many times he heard it, or how much he saw, Krystian wasn't sure he'd ever get use to the knowledge of things outside of the norm.

"So your aunt, who happens to be very dead, has been helping you understand your gifts?"

"Yup. That about sums it up."

They both sat there in silence for a moment. Krystian was trying to accept what she'd just told him, and Reign was trying to figure out where he'd planned on taking the conversation after their small talk.

"This is good," he said, after taking a sip from his glass. "What is it?"

"A warm butterscotch mulled cider hot totty I started making before you got here. I needed something to take the edge off."

Then they both fell silent again. The tension was so thick in the air that it was making Krystian rethink his entire purpose for stopping by. He wanted to explain about his brother, his father, and even how much he regretted not being honest with her from the beginning. But now, being in her presence, everything changed.

"Look Reign," he began, "I know how uncomfortable things were the other day. I just really wanted to talk to you and clear things up."

"There's really nothing left to clear up. Whatever we could have had is in the past, and I'm not sure we can ever get that back...."

"But that's the thing," Krystian interrupted, "I did a lot of thinking, and I don't want it back."

Reign's expression revealed the surprise his words caused. Surely he didn't pop up over her house at the cusp of dusk to tell her he was no longer interested. There was no way he was sitting there, looking like his world had fallen apart, only to tell her that he was letting go.

"You don't?"

"No. I want the life where you know all of my dirty horrible and embarrassing secrets, and you tell me how you can read my mind and mix cocktails in the dark. I want...no, I *need* to have the amazing woman that I ended up having the worst date of my life with back *in* my life."

Reign was speechless. She halfway expected some sappy sad apology, but nothing like this. At that moment, the honesty and intensity that she saw in his eyes was the only thing that left her grasping for a reality and normalcy that she no longer had.

So they sat there, staring at one another with the candles still flickering brightly, neither of them knowing what to say next. But Krystian didn't need words. He leaned in close, cupped her face in his hands and kissed her long and sweet.

"I should have done that quite a while ago," he finally said. "I don't know why it took me so long."

Reign looked at him, lost for thought and words. Here he was, the man that had plagued her entire existence since the day they met, and at last he'd kissed her. But all she could think about was how she'd wish he hadn't. It wasn't her emotions that left Reign feeling so put off; it was what she felt when his lips touched hers. An intense chill that she could not shake set deep in her bones.

As much as she knew something was off, Reign couldn't deny the whirlwind of emotions he made her feel. And how kissing him had left her wanting more.

"Yeah, you probably should have, then maybe things wouldn't have gotten so volatile between us."

"I don't think a kiss could have covered up the fact that I lied by not telling you everything."

Krystian leaned back on the couch and pulled her with him. He never thought that he'd be holding Reign in his arms again. He never missed anything so much in his life.

"You smell good," he said while she leaned back in his arms. "Not like the lavender and jasmine that you use to wear all the time, but still good."

"It's this sage and lemon that..." Reign stopped mid-sentence. *Dominic bought for me.*

Just when she thought there might be some normalcy taking form in her romantic life, she remembered the intense and impossibly sapphire blue eyes of Dominic Amoureux. And now, things were more complicated than ever.

"That what?"

"Krys, I have to tell you something."

He stopped her, because whatever she had to tell him could wait. Krystian didn't want to ruin the moment that had taken them so long to get to. He just wanted to indulge in it a little longer before having to return to reality.

"I think whatever you have to tell me can wait until tomorrow," he interjected. "I would much rather kiss you again."

Reign sat up then turned and looked at him. He was leaning back into the sofa so comfortably, and in his eyes she could see the flicker of everything he felt for her. Reign had lain on his chest and looked up at him, his face just inches from hers.

"Kissing is the only thing on your mind?"

"No," he smiled, "but there's a mood now."

"Well I thought there was supposed to be a *mood* for these kinds of things. Or am I mistaken?"

"For most people, you're probably right. But for us, not so much," Krystian stated matter of factly.

"Please explain," she implored.

"Reign, right now I'd like nothing more than to lay you on that bed in there," he began, nodding toward her bedroom door, "then kiss and touch every inch of you until you lost all control. Then make sure every one of your senses were consumed by me."

Reign felt her breath quicken at the thought, and her skin was hot like fire. "So, why don't you?"

"Because, as I said, there's a mood. A mood or a moment isn't what I want with you. I don't want you to wake up thinking 'what the hell did I just do'. I want to wake up to you asking me to do it again," he answered, then kissed her on the lips.

"And again," Reign added, kissing him back.

"You're really good at emphasis I see."

"Yeah, it's a new power that I picked up," she said with a smile.

Krystian had more that he needed to discuss with Reign, but he was so content with her lying in his arms and wasn't quite ready to ruin the moment. So, the potentially life altering news that he had planned on sharing with her would have to wait just a bit longer.

As Reign laid there with Krystian holding her, she wasn't as at ease as he was. Yes, she was happy being with him in this intimate way, but so much had happened in the past few months; so much had changed. And she knew that he was out for his father, but if it came down to saving her life or taking Donovan's, what would Krystian choose? How deep did his hatred for his father run?

And she couldn't forget about Dominic. His kindness, generosity and concern had won her over; with his physical beauty only adding to it.

Feeling his breathing become rhythmic, she knew he had fallen asleep. But Reign couldn't, she was restless, and still hadn't been given the moment she needed to process everything that had happened within the past day, let alone month. Then Krystian squeezed her gently in his arms, almost like he knew her mind was racing. Reign gave in; convincing herself that tonight she'd stop thinking...stop worrying for just a moment and indulge in what she had now. There'd be enough time for fretting, explaining, and figuring out tomorrow. Right now, she was content with her momentary peace.

When Reign woke, the sun was just cresting over the horizon. Looking up at Krystian she had a flash of déjà vu. It seemed like forever ago since the first night he'd slept over. Back then she was running from the monsters in her dreams, which these days came at her during all times of the day. But at least now, with the warding complete, she'd be safe in her own home.

Krystian didn't move when she pushed herself up. He looked exhausted, like he'd been through hell and back. And with that thought, all of the worries came flooding back. They had to talk and have a real conversation before he left.

Heading to her room, Reign's next thought was to take an extremely hot shower; but when she stepped through the doorway she was no longer in her house.

"No, no, no ,no. This is not happening. I'm protected in my home."

She had no idea where she was, but it looked like a warehouse, and she could smell and hear the lap of saltwater nearby.

"Hello," Reign called out, but was only met with her echo.

It was dark and didn't have that other worldly feel like when Nicola was invading her mind. So, she began walking aimlessly in the dark. After about ten minutes Reign heard voices, but she didn't think she recognized any of them.

"I told you to take care of her before! I knew she'd be a problem," one of the voices shouted.

"It's not that simple. She can do these *things*…it doesn't even make sense," came another voice.

Reign continued walking until she saw light illuminating the outline of a door. She quietly moved toward it, listening intently.

"When I sent you there the first time, was she doing all of these things? Maybe that's how she managed to *not* be dead right now!," came the first voice again.

Reign got the impression that this guy was the boss of the two.

"I don't know how she managed to survive. She was cold and dead when I left."

It was then that Reign finally realized what she was listening to. Her murderer was having a conversation with whomever put the hit out on her *about* her. But how did they know about her abilities? Next to no one had a clue about what she was capable of doing, and those that did she trusted with her life not to tell a soul.

Reign was about to reach for the doorknob but froze when the footsteps and voices started getting closer.

"Look," the boss said, "I don't care how it gets done, but this *problem* needs to be resolved quickly."

"And what about her boyfriend?"

There was a long pause before the boss replied.

"If he gets in the way…," he said with a heavy sigh, "then he must be taken care of as well. Anyone who gets in the way, *take care of them.*"

Then Reign had a moment of panic as the doorknob turned the door began to open. The light that came through the gaping doorway was so blindingly bright that Reign couldn't make out the faces of the men that exited, and not only that, but they couldn't see her either.

"Good morning sleepy head," Krystian said looking down at her.

Reign's head popped up, completely unaware of where she was.

"Are you okay?" he asked. "You look like you just had a bad dream."

Sitting up, Reign tried to get her bearings. When she remembered where she was, she finally spoke.

"Not a dream, a vision."

"Like the one you had at your dad's?" Krystian asked.

"Yes and no. This one was completely unprovoked, but the one at my dad's was triggered when I touched the doorknob," she responded.

"You don't look so good. I'm gonna get you something to drink," he said, getting off the couch and heading to the kitchen.

"Believe it or not, I actually feel worse than I look," then Reign paused when she remembered what she'd heard. "Shit," she mumbled into her cupped hands.

"What? What is it?" he asked, handing her a nice sized cup of orange juice.

"I need everyone here. Dad, Alexa, Adrian, James, Lisa…and Dominic."

Krystian was reaching into his pocket for his phone when he paused. "Dominic? Who's that?"

"I'll explain everything later. But right now, I just need everyone that's important to me here. It literally is a matter of life and death."

Chapter 17

It was a little after noon, and Reign was now seated at her dining room table surrounded by the seven people that mattered the most to her: Julien, Alexa, Lisa, Adrian, James, Krystian, and Dominic. And of them, only Dominic and James had no clue as to who Reign was or the things that she could do, but she had to tell them. All of their lives depended on the choices *she* made, so there could not be any secrets.

"Thank you all so much for coming," Reign began. "First things first. I want to introduce you to someone that you've heard about, but never had the pleasure of meeting."

Reign looked at Dominic, who had taken the seat directly across from her.

"This is Detective Dominic Amoureux...."

"You saved mô fiy," Julien interrupted then stood and walked toward Dominic, his face full with sentiment. "Please, this is all I need to know to welcome you."

Dominic was taken off guard when Julien grasped his hand firmly. But even so, he stood without hesitation and accepted the warm embrace of a grateful father.

Reign sat in silence, overcome by the emotional moment her father displayed and the way Dominic humbly, and without question, accepted his show of gratitude.

"So this is him?" Alexa spoke up once Julien had returned to his seat. Then she gave Reign a knowing glance.

Sighing heavily, Reign continued.

"This is Dominic Amoureux, and yes this is the him that saved my life."

"Well, now I see why you never wanted me," James blurted without thinking. Then averted his eyes at Lisa's sharp glare.

"Please, this isn't a time for jokes, drama or otherwise. There are some things that I need to say. Like literal life hanging in the balance things."

As she spoke, Reign was fully aware of the stare Krystian was boring into her skull from his seat next to her. And she just as purposefully refused to look in his direction.

"There are some things that most of you know about me. And specifically for James and Dominic, there are quite a few things that you definitely need to know. But I'm a firm believer in: the best way to tell you...is to show you."

Closing her eyes, Reign focused all of her thoughts on the things that Tempest had shown her the day before. She'd never attempted to telepathically link a feeling, let alone a flood of thoughts, to anyone before. But if she could do this, it would serve two purposes. Not only did she need to enlighten those that didn't know about her gifts, but she also had to inform the others of the things she'd learned in recent months.

"I need each of you to clear your minds and trust me," Reign said, outstretching her hands and turning her palms face up. Then she began repeating rhythmically, "*Monstrare quod video, da illis a vision, per meos oculos.*"

All attention was on her. Not one person at the table could take their eyes off Reign as she continued with the chant. Even Julien, who was still quite powerful, was drawn into her seemingly melodic mantra.

As everyone focused on Reign, they became lulled and hypnotized by her chant. With eyes still closed, she could feel when each person at the table connected into the circle. Then, when Reign sensed she had control over them all, her entranced eyes flew open, revealing clear crystalline irises.

Immediately and without warning, everyone's vision grew hazy then changed. It was like they were third party to the revelation Reign had had with Tempest, only they saw it through her eyes. Nicola's betrayal of her sister, the manipulation of their father and the attempt at bringing the Moreau line to an end.

Almost an hour later they still sat there. Bewitched by Reign's spell, they bore witness to the relentless greed of a father and ultimate betrayal of a sister. When it was done, one by one, they were all released from the vision. Once everyone was freed they sat in silence for a moment; unable to speak and attempting to comprehend everything that they had just seen.

Julien was the first one to speak. "This is all my family's fault? Nicola tried bring an entire line to an end."

Even though Reign had already spoken to him about the things she'd learned, it was altogether different to experience it firsthand. And now that he had, Julien was unable to shake the guilt that had overcome him.

"Don't do that. *She* tried to end an entire line," Reign interjected. "None of this has anything to do with you, and the worst of it happened before either of us were even born. So, if you can blame yourself, so can I."

Julien looked up at her with a surprised expression. "There's no reason you should feel blame at all. You are the most innocent in all of this."

"My point exactly," Reign said with a knowing look. "We are not the sins of our parents, we are each of our own mind and soul."

"So, what are you?" James asked, interrupting the exchange between father and daughter. "I'm sorry, I don't know any other way to say it. You just took control over my mind and made me see things. Are you some kind of witch?"

"I am, what you would call, a kado avék maji legacy. My father is too. Our family is rooted in the African Voodoun religion, but we're also born with gifts."

Reign paused for a moment. The majority of what she was about to share with the people surrounding her she had learned from Tempest. The task of their family's ancestral tracing had ended with what Tempest had been taught by Aiyana, so not even Reign's father knew all of their history.

"What kinds of gifts," James questioned.

"My father and I come from a very old tribe in East Africa called the Angaza Tribe. My ancestor Asha was, what could have been called, a Queen. She'd been born with abilities that no one before her had ever seen, which included seeing spirits and having glimpses of the future. One night she had a dream that, four generations from her own, the tribe would go to war with and be in jeopardy of extinction at the hands of a foreign land. She shared with no one what she had seen, but knew something had to be done.

"Throughout previous years Asha sought out spirits for their otherworldly knowledge. So, using what she'd learned, she called on her ancestors for protection. But because it was only her blood-line Asha could influence, she was made to take on a second name to give them distinction. That's where the surname Chidike came from. And no matter if it was man or woman, anyone born into Asha's bloodline would have to take on, and continue, the name.

"Now inclined to learn, practice and pass down sacred tribal magick, the Chidike's of the Anganza Tribe had become strong enough to fight off their long-awaited enemies. But, as with everything given time, their gifts inadvertently evolved into something greater.

"There soon came another magick source. The Chidike's began calling them natural gifts, which are abilities unique to the individual. Usually they begin to manifest around the thirteenth birthday, give or take. By ancestral law, these gifts cannot be stolen or passed down."

"So, is that what your *sixth sense* was growing up?" Alexa asked, intrigued by what she was learning about her friend. "Your gifted magic?"

"Yes," Reign answered with a smile. "Now, while our natural gifts strengthen and develop over time, legacy abilities grow stronger and stronger with each offspring. We can receive this ancestral knowledge at any time by performing three separate spirit ceremonies, but it's never at fullest potential until our Chidike-born parent dies."

All at once everyone turned to look at Julien.

"It is a part of who we are," he said simply. "These ceremonies that pass down magick also serve as a conduit to keep us anchored to our blood in death and vice versa. It is a comforting thing."

Reign smiled at her father. She was so thankful that when had been broken between them was now, for the most part, repaired. He was the only person left alive that could even remotely understand her plight.

"I'm telling all of you this because I had a vision last night," Reign continued. "I feel like, on that in-between the lines scale, there's a warning. And anyone close to me, anyone I love, can get caught in the crossfire."

She then looked at Krystian before continuing. This next part would probably be the hardest to swallow, but she had to get it over with.

"There is also another element to all of this. The man that my father was hired to work for, who also happens to be the man that wants me dead as a result, is Krystian's father."

Everyone, except Adrian, was staring at him now. Feeling backed into a preverbal corner, Krystian looked everyone. No longer afraid of what others thought, he maintained eye contact with everyone and began speaking. He was his father's son, not his father.

"Yes Donovan, my father, is the one that hired Julien and put a hit out on Reign," Krystian began then paused for a moment; he knew he had to continue and lay it all out. "My father and I haven't spoken to each other in almost five years. I couldn't get past the things he'd done and the man he'd become, so I came down here to put an end to it all when I realized he had made contact with Julien. He's ruined a lot of lives and I wanted to cease his threat."

Krystian said the last sentence while looking at Reign. He could tell she was still torn over the whole 'his father wanted her dead' bit. But he wasn't going to let that happen, nor was he ever going to give her a reason to question her trust for him again.

As Reign sat there in silence and Krystian continued to talk about Donovan, she started feeling restless. Clenching her fists, she shifted in her seat to try and get more comfortable. Suddenly, Reign couldn't hear anything Krystian was saying, although she continued to sit there calmly. She hoped that whatever she was experiencing wasn't another vision, and would quickly pass.

"Calm down and breathe," Reign heard the words as if someone was talking directly into her ear. "It's going to be ok, just take a deep breath and relax."

Wherever the voice came from, she seemed to be the only one who could hear it.

"I need you to stay cool and listen to me. It's Dominic."

Reign's looked in his direction, but he was so absorbed in the conversation going on that she doubted what she was hearing.

"I've been doing this for a while, so I may not appear to be focused on you, but believe me I am. I have gifts too, and this is one of them. We really need to talk....alone. Can you make that happen?"

Having never done anything like this before, Reign didn't know how to answer him without opening her mouth. Looking back at Dominic, she could see him crack a smile.

"Just...smile if you can make it happen. I love when you smile."

And Reign did just that...she smiled.

By the time Reign had gotten the house clear, it was six o'clock in the evening. They'd talked, ate and laughed for hours, which was just what had been needed to lighten the mood of a very intense discussion. It felt good to finally have the air clear. Krystian no longer had the guilt of who his father was weighing on him, and she could be herself...around everyone that mattered to her.

Of course, there was still the matter of Dominic, who was currently making his way back to her house. Even though Reign was in a sharing kind of mood she still wanted to keep him to herself. And besides that, she was very interested in learning more about his abilities and why he found it necessary to share them with her.

The doorbell rang just as she was loading the last of the dishes in the dishwasher.

"Just a sec," she called out.

When Reign opened the door Dominic was standing there just as she'd expected. Reign wondered if she'd ever get over how completely beautiful he was. His dark hair was such a contrast to his piercing light eyes, and it was unsettling.

"What is that," she asked, noting the bag in his hands.

"Well, I figured that with all of the secret sharing today you probably need something to help you wind down," he said with a grin while walking through the door.

As Reign headed to the living room and sat on the sofa he walked past her and straight to the kitchen. Taking two glasses out of the cabinet, Dominic poured a generous amount of the golden amber liquid that was cloaked by a plastic bag.

"What is it?" Reign asked when he handed her the glass.

"Taste it first and then I'll tell you," he replied, taking a seat next to her.

Reign took a sniff, then a small sip.

"Okay, now will you tell me what is this?"

"Butterscotch whisky. Never had it before in my life, but I thought it would be nice to try something new with you."

Taking another sip from her glass, Reign remembered what had happened the last time they were alone and alcohol had been involved. *But it's so good*, she thought to herself, and took another sip.

Dominic took the opportunity that was given to him and looked at her face. The bruises had faded drastically and the cut that was above her eye from the fall was now very shallow, and only slightly noticeable.

"Do you trust me?"

Reign was caught completely off guard by his question. And truth be told, the effects of the whisky was beginning to quickly creep up on her.

"Yes," she answered cautiously.

Then, without hesitation, Dominic cupped his hand over the shallow bruise he was just assessing. Reign felt her forehead tingle for a moment where his hand was, then there was nothing.

Feeling her head where his hand had just been, Reign felt no sign of the cut. She had become very self-conscious of the scar that had been left behind, and so, was always touching it. The mark was a painful reminder of what had almost happened.

Getting up, Reign walked to her bedroom bathroom and looked in the mirror. What she saw left her astounded.

"How did you do that?" she asked in amazement when Dominic entered behind her.

"I told you, I have gifts too."

Continuing to stare at her reflection, Reign could see that the scar was completely gone. Not even a shallow trace of the gash that was there just moments ago was left.

"But how…"

Reign was speechless, not knowing what to say or ask. She'd never been aware of anyone with any kind of natural abilities outside of her family.

"I had an idea when we were back at Eden, but today is when I was sure."

"Sure of what," she asked, turning to face him.

Taking a deep breath Dominic paused for a moment. He wanted her to know everything, but was fighting with himself if he should.

"Do you remember the story I told you about my great-great grandfather and Justine Baptiste?"

"Yes," Reign answered, now becoming aware of the intimacy of their closeness and surroundings. They were in the bathroom of her *bedroom* of all places, and only standing inches apart. This was definitely not the most ideal situation for either of them.

Apparently Dominic was thinking the same thing, because before continuing, he took her hand and led her back to the living room. Then he refilled their glasses and handed hers to her.

"You're probably going to need this to get through what I'm about to tell you."

Reign took the glass, and another sip, then patiently waited for him to continue.

"Justine was very *open* with my granpa. There were no secrets between them," he began. "That's how he knew about her gifts and being an enlightened one. However, they very wisely kept all of this guarded carefully between themselves, especially since people like her had been highly sought out by local covens.

"When Justine was murdered, a coven was attempting to steal her powers, but they never succeeded. When I told you that she turned to look and my granpa before taking her last breath, it wasn't just to take one last look at him. It was to bequeath him her gifts with her final breath."

Reign sat there, just as shaken and emotional as when Dominic had first told her the story. It was like a great tragedy, Justine and Dominic's love. And for her to trust him with something so sacred, that was the ultimate proclamation of her feelings.

"So, that's where your gifts came from?" Reign concluded.

"Yes. It passed down and manifested in the first-born male of each generation." Dominic said with a hesitant smile. "But there's just one thing that you're missing."

"What?"

"After Justine died, she came to granpa quite a few times to help him understand the gifts that she had given him. During those visits she revealed a great deal of information, which included the fact that she too came from a powerful African line. She also told him that his family would be charged with protecting her magic until our line and hers reunited."

Reign had a hunch that she knew where the conversation was going, and she did not like it. Finishing off her glass she was feeling very warm and relaxed physically, but continued to focus on him.

"When you told us your story today, it was like reality had finally set in. I mean, I knew the truth of my granpa's words, but I honestly doubted I would ever run into the distant relative of his only true love. It seemed like something more suited to be considered lore than fact."

"And you think that I share blood with Justine?"

"I don't think, I know it. The only way you were able to hear me was because you are of Justine's blood; that was the sign."

Reign sat there for a moment in deep thought before continuing. "And you're telling me that her power that was bestowed to the Amoureux's now must somehow be transferred to me?" she asked.

"Yes, that's exactly what I'm saying."

All she could do was sit there in total disbelief. Was this the reason she had been so drawn to him when they'd first met? Were her feelings for him simply tied to a centuries old prophecy? Then something else dawned on her.

"Wait. So, if taking those powers from Justine was lethal to her, what will it do to you?"

"Yeah, about that...."

Reign didn't bother letting him finish before jumping up from her seat. "Yeah, you can *forget* that. Unless we can find a way around you *dying*, you can forget about fulfilling your destiny."

When she got up and began to pace the living room he stood and walked over to her. When Dominic was in front of her she quickly turned her head.

"Look at me," he said, then cupped and turned Reign's chin so she would face him.

When she looked into his eyes, he couldn't believe what he saw. She was crying. It bothered Dominic that he was the cause of her tears, but he didn't know what to do about it. Sure he would've liked to tell her that her love was the key to saving him but he couldn't, and wouldn't, put that kind of pressure on her. And from the glances he noticed that were passed between her and Krystian earlier, Reign's heart already belonged to another.

"I'm sorry, I just can't do this. No matter what I do or don't do, someone I care about is the one that has to suffer. I'm just so tired of it."

If they were standing there, locked in the same intense gaze under any other circumstances, Dominic would have shared with her everything he was feeling. And it took every bit of self-control he had not to kiss Reign's tear streaked face until her pain turned to passion. Yes, he *needed* her to love him if he were to survive what returning Justine's power would do to him. But the more Dominic got to know her the more he *wanted* her to love him.

"You know, I should probably be going. It looks like that whisky is starting to take its toll on you," he said, breaking their spell.

Dominic's words caused her heart to drop, because just like before, he rejected her. Of course, that was probably a good thing considering she had just been lip locking with Krystian earlier that day.

"Yeah, you're right. I should probably go and sleep this off," Reign replied.

Dominic took the glasses and put them in the kitchen sink, then she walked him to the door. Reign didn't want him to leave, but she knew if he stayed any longer she'd stop thinking with her brain and give in to what she was feeling.

"So, we should probably get together soon," Dominic finally said.

"Yeah, probably. But I'm still not so sure about what you're saying. It's just..."

"We'll talk about it later," he said, cutting her off. "There's more to think about than just you and I here."

Dominic stood there, staring at Reign for another uncomfortable minute. If only they'd met first...but it wasn't his time. And if by some miracle she did end up falling in love with him, he couldn't tell her everything until he was sure it was the right thing to do.

"I'm beginning to feel like some vigilante martyr," Reign sighed.

Smiling at the very accurate description of her life, Dominic gave a little smile, then leaned down and kissed her on the nose.

"I'll be working all day tomorrow and Wednesday, but I'll give you a call and we can figure out when is good for you to meet up again."

"Yeah, okay," she said softly before he turned and walked out the door.

Once Dominic was gone, Reign headed to the bedroom, turning out the lights along the way. She couldn't deny the love she had for Krystian, and that everything he made her feel was unlike anything she'd ever experienced. But with Dominic it was something different. Even though now that she knew a family connection existed, there was still something else that drew them together. She couldn't bear the thought of him dying just to give her some power that her great-great-great-great gave his great-great-great-great.

Not bothering to shower or change, Reign just pulled off her sweatpants and climbed into bed. Today had drained her on so many levels, and at that moment, all she wanted to do was sleep.

Chapter 18

It was about ten o'clock Tuesday morning when Reign woke up. She hadn't planned on going in to the gallery, but she needed something to do to occupy her mind. And even though it was apparent that she wasn't going to see Dominic, he still weighed heavily on her mind. Krystian however, she would possibly be seeing, though that wouldn't happen until later in the day.

Reign had been thinking about the night Dominic had saved her. All the power and training she had and still wasn't able to fend off a drunken man. So, she'd been practicing with Sato Sensei during most of her periods of down time and dedicating hours each evening to meditation.

Reign was becoming antsy, and she knew it. She needed a way to exert her pent-up energy beside kicking and punching a bag; she wanted to hit something, or *someone*, that sorely deserved it. Still buried deep down in the covers,

Reign looked up at the closet door. The bodysuit that she'd impulsively purchased a few days before was hanging there.

"I am not a damn superhero," she mumbled aloud and closed her eyes.

Two seconds later she received a text notification. It was from Alexa. *Are you free to go dress hunting today? I was thinking Madame Beauregard's at noonish?*

Yeah, sounds great. I'll meet you there. She text back.

Since having a lazy day under the covers was now no longer an option, Reign rolled out of bed. And as she headed into the bathroom to start getting ready for the day, she gave the bodysuit one final glance.

"That dress looks amazing on you," Lisa said when Alexa exited the dressing room wearing a silk and lace belle styled wedding gown.

"You said that about the last four dresses," Reign sighed. "If you don't stop being so overly agreeable she's never going to pick a dress."

Alexa rolled her eyes and gave a little laugh at Reign's comment. "I can't help it that I happen to look amazing in everything."

"And Ms. Vain Jane just proved my point," Reign replied, taking a sip from her wine glass.

"So, what colors are ya'll going with? That'll help us narrow down the dress," Lisa asked.

"Burgundy and silver with royal blue accents," Alexa answered.

Reign looked from Alexa to Lisa, and then glanced around shop. "Give me a second," she said, before heading into the sea of lace, silk and taffeta that filled the shop.

When Reign returned to their private room fifteen minutes later, Lisa and Alexa were sitting down talking and sipping their wine.

"I think I've found it," Reign announced, displaying the gown draped over her arms.

The consultant that was helping them took the dress from Reign and hung it on the dressing room door for Alexa to try on.

"So, I've been meaning to ask," Lisa began, "what is up with you and Mr. Sexy?"

Reign looked at her in complete confusion.

"She means Dominic," Alexa chimed in from within the changing room.

"Nothing," Reign answered, "he's just a really good guy that happened to have saved my life. He's also the lead detective working on Mrs. Renaud's case."

At the thought of Reign's kindly neighbor, all three women grew quiet for a minute. None of them said it, but for a fleeting moment the reality of current circumstances hit them with full force.

"Well he seemed to be more than nothing yesterday. The air was so heavy between you two I thought we were all going to suffocate," Lisa added, breaking the uncomfortable silence.

"First Krystian, now Dominic. Girl what are you going to do?" Alexa asked.

Finally, Reign spoke up. "Can I be completely honest?"

"Please do," Lisa and Alexa said at the same time.

Reign smiled and took a long drink from her wine glass, which their consultant magically kept filled. She hadn't been able to spend quality time like this with her friends in a while, so these precious moments meant a lot to her.

"I have no clue what I'm doing. Before Krystian and I fell out, he was everything to me, so considering another man wouldn't have even been an option."

"So what changed?" Lisa asked.

"Well, aside from Krys's omissions of truth…those two days I spent with Dominic. Not only did he save my life, but in the span of twenty-four hours he shared so much of himself."

"You bonded with him," Alexa said, pausing. "You've lost a lot, and are still missing out on considerable amount. By him sharing so much, that allowed you to kind of *fill in your gaps*."

Reign had never thought of it like that. And with his recent revelation, Alexa's logic *did* make sense. But it still didn't make her situation any less problematic.

"Ladies," Alexa said breaking the silence as she exited the dressing room with a huge smile.

"Wow," was the only word Lisa could get out.

The gown Reign had picked was silk and cut in a mermaid silhouette with a sweetheart neckline. The asymmetrical knee length hemline was lengthened by an abundant taffeta flounce. But the real eye catcher was the ruby red appliques that had been sewn into the train of taffeta and brooch at the hemline.

"Yeah, wow," Reign agreed.

"I think we have a winner," Alexa said with a glow that Reign had never seen before.

Both Lisa and Reign stood up and walked over to her friend, then hugged her tight. When they all started crying, Alexa pulled away.

"Oh no no no no, we're not doing this. It's time to find bridesmaid dresses for you two. I need ya'll looking and feeling just as fabulous. No way am I going to be the jealous bride and have my girls looking like a fashion catastrophe."

Alexa watched her two friends as they tried on gown after gown. And for those few hours they talked, laughed and drank as though they had no other concern in the world. Planning a wedding was just the distraction they needed to add a little normalcy to their lives, and each of them was glad for it.

"So, when did Adrian and Krystian decide to make James a thing?" Reign asked as the women exited Madame Beauregard's.

"Sometime after the dinner party a few days ago. Something about them needing to form a brotherhood to our alliance," Lisa answered.

Reign burst into laughter. "Our alliance? They make us sound so...*official*."

"Well we are," Alexa said, feigning offence. "Have you seen us?"

"Speaking of alliances," Reign began, "how are things going with you and James?"

Lisa smiled as they crossed the street. They were headed to a nearby bistro to meet Krystian, Adrian and James for a late lunch.

"He is amazing. Seriously, how could you *not have* fallen for him Reign?"

"I agree, James is a catch. But I just guess he wasn't for me. I was never drawn to him like..." Reign suddenly stopped herself. Every time she was faced with the realization of her dilemma, the weight of her entire life came crashing down.

"Krys and Dominic. Go ahead, you can say it," Alexa said in a comforting tone.

"Yeah, Krys and Dominic. It's almost like, since I had a taste of this vintage, aged, sweet, full bodied wine...my palate could never accept this five year old Riesling, no matter how exclusive it may be considered to be."

"Leave it up to you to make a comparison like this solely using wine," Lisa laughed. "But I get it, I do. James is *my* vintage."

"There they are," Alexa smiled picking up her pace.

When the group entered the doors of La Terrain de Marécage Bistro, they were seated almost immediately.

"Well, they have great service, I'll give them that," Lisa complimented.

"So, I have a confession to make," Adrian began once they were all situated. "I haven't mentioned it to my lovely fiancée yet, but I'm considering this establishment to cater the wedding. And not only that, but I would be honored to have all of you to choose the menu."

Everyone was so surprised by this announcement that no one said a word, not even Alexa.

"Please stop looking at me as if I just grew another head," he added.

"Okay, before I give in to the overwhelming excitement I'm feeling, I'm going to wait for Lex's reaction," Reign said, "because I obviously can't love the idea if she hates it."

Alexa looked at Adrian, placed her hands on either side of his face, then gave him the biggest kiss.

"Ok, yes, yes, yes...I love the idea. And I'd love to try whatever food you plan on putting in front of me!" Reign exclaimed.

"So how does this work?" Krystian asked, while smiling from Reign's obvious excitement. "You put a few choices in front of us and we taste everything?"

"No. Order whatever you want and think might taste good, from wine to dinner, to dessert. The wedding menu will consist of a choice of each from every person."

"So, the menu will have four choices of everything?" James asked.

"No, six. My lovely fiancée and I will be making a selection as well. And enjoy every bite, I'm picking up the tab as well," Adrian added.

"My girl got a winner too," Reign mumbled loud enough for everyone to hear.

Krystian looked at her, curious about the comment she'd just made. Feeling his stare, Reign turned to look at him.

"Krys, we've been through a lot, and I mean *a lot*. I've been thinking about you and us lately and if I am to be honest, I know you never set out to hurt me. But the timing was so off. Being flooded with these abilities, my father coming back into my life, losing Paw Paw…it all took such a toll on me."

"So, what are you trying to say?" He asked when Reign paused, seemingly unable to continue.

"I think we should work through whatever our past issues were and see if we could make something out of this…this *thing* that we have," she said with finality.

Looking at him, her insides were in knots. Her heart told her that everything she felt for Krystian was love. Her mind told her she couldn't very well love two people, so what she was feeling for Dominic had to be something else. And she wasn't willing to lose love over what could possibly be lust, or something else.

Krystian leaned over to Reign and kissed her deeply, happy to finally be able to express his feelings for her openly. And she kissed him just as intensely, but there was a piece of her heart that left her mind wondering, was she making the right choice?

It was going on seven o'clock when, at last, Reign was headed home. Krystian had given her a few not so subtle hints that he wanted to stop by, and as much as Reign wanted to see him, she had to postpone his request.

As the evening had begun to wind down, one thought had continued to repeatedly intruded Reign's mind: Mrs. Renaud. She remembered when her gifts were just beginning to develop; she had stopped by her father's and had a vision which was prompted from touching his doorknob. Then there was the vision she'd had one morning at home and later realized that it was triggered by a tiny drop of blood that she'd stepped on.

Reign wasn't completely familiar with the realm of her abilities, but she had a notion that she couldn't quite shake. If she could get into Mrs. Renaud's house, maybe she could initiate another vision by touching things. It wasn't exactly a science, but Reign had nothing else to go on.

Once Reign arrived home, she immediately headed into her bedroom and pulled the bodysuit from its hanger on the door.

"This is completely ridiculous," she mumbled to herself. "Yeah but what if I could help solve Granny's murder...doesn't she deserve that much?"

Tears welled in her eyes from the thought of the sweet lady she'd know for over nine years being harmed. Reign was sure Mrs. Renaud had never hurt a soul in her life, and there was no way she deserved what had happened to her. *Someone* had to pay; she could not allow this to be another one of those ghost cases that went on, unsolved forever.

Now fully dressed, Reign slipped on the black tabi boots that she'd gotten when Sato Sensei had first begun training her. He said that they weren't necessary, but she had to have them.

Looking out of her bedroom window, Reign could see that night had completely fallen. Since there was no way for her to gauge the length of any one vision, she didn't want to go over there too late, but it needed to be dark. So, after taking several deep breaths she grabbed the spare key given to her by Mrs. Renaud after her husband died, and headed out the back door.

Reign had unlocked the door to Mrs. Renaud's screened in back porch and was now standing in the entryway to the den rethinking her impetuous decision. She hadn't considered the effect walking around the cold, dark and empty house would have on her. So now, with the anger and adrenaline gone, she was faced with the possible error of her decision.

Then another realization came to her. There was the very likely possibility that she may be the only person capable of finding the killer. She was positive that if the police had any lead whatsoever, Dominic would have surely told her. So, after taking a deep breath, Reign continued on through the threshold.

It may have been late summer in New Orleans, but the house did in fact feel eerily cold. Reign didn't know if it was her spirit or gifts reacting to the violent energy that remained, but either way, it left her full of emotion.

Reign could tell by the displays on the electronics that the electricity was still on, but the last thing she wanted to do was turn the lights on and alert any passer byers to her presence.

"Illuminé," she whispered.

She'd done a few short meditations with Sylvie over the past couple of days. Learning to redirect her energy with simple commands versus concentrating her thoughts or saying entire chants was an accomplishment worth mentioning. And right now, she was very thankful for it.

"In certain circumstances, you wouldn't have the time to focus and convey. That's where learning verbal redirection would come in and be quite handy," Sylvie had told her.

"More expensive night vision goggles huh," Reign whispered, referring to how much brighter and clearer things were now as opposed to the first time she'd done it.

Taking a moment to walk around the house, Reign took in her surroundings. Nothing was out of place or missing, but nonetheless the air felt wrong. She went into the upstairs bedroom, which still carried the faint scent of peppermint from the oil Mrs. Renaud had sworn by. When she'd descended the stairs and re-entered the living room, Reign smiled at the picture she'd given the couple upon purchasing the Vieux.

Standing there for a moment longer, Reign had to face the fact that she was procrastinating. It's not like she wanted to see what happened, and for all she knew her plan wouldn't work at all. But the unknown of everything is what scared her the most. The possibility of what she would, *or wouldn't*, find.

Reign walked around the house attempting to locate where she felt the strongest energy. It only took her one walk through the house to realize that being in the living room stirred her spirit the most. And that is where she now stood, gathering her strength while preparing for the indefinite.

Kneeling down and placing both of her hands on the floor, Reign then closed her eyes.

"Revelet deus absconsa tua," she whispered.

Immediately Reign's vision went dark. However, she remained calm and trusted her gifts as Tempest had instructed her. Within a few seconds the veil of darkness began to lift, as if a rising curtain to a play. Focusing her thoughts on what she wanted to see, Mrs. Renaud appeared before her eyes.

"Yes, may I help you?" she said, answering the knock at the door.

It was pitch black, and Reign could see that Mrs. Renaud was moving about with a flashlight in hand.

"Good evening ma'am. I was wondering if I could use your phone. I'm here to pay a visit your neighbor next door, but no one seems to be home and I stupidly forgot my cell phone," a voice answered.

"Oh, you must mean my Reign. She's always in and out," Mrs. Renaud replied with a bright smile.

"So you know her then?" the voice asked.

"Yes, she's very sweet that one. Just like a granddaughter to me too," she continued, moving to the side to let him in. "Well come on in. Please don't mind the darkness; I'm hoping Entergy gets this power back on soon."

No, don't let him in, Reign pleaded in her head. *He's dangerous.*

Then it happened without warning. The moment Mrs. Renaud turned her back to lock the front door, the strange man hit her on the back of the head with something, causing her to collapse to the floor. He picked her up, carried her limp body to the sofa and laid her down. He then pulled a chair up, staring at her until she began to stir.

"What happened?" Mrs. Renaud asked after a few minutes, as she rubbed the back of her head.

"You collapsed. I tried to catch you, but couldn't get to you quick enough."

She sat there for a moment thinking, then finally looked up at him with frightened wide eyes.

"No, I didn't fall. You hit me!"

Reign saw when she tried to scream, but he clamped his hand over her mouth before she could. And his face, it was so shrouded in darkness that she couldn't make out a single distinct feature. He was like a shadow moving throughout the vision.

"You don't want to do that, because if you do, your precious Reign will be the next casualty," he practically sneered.

From that moment things happened so quickly. He feigned remorse and let her go. Unfortunately, by the time she made it to the door, he was right behind her. Reign saw the glint from a knife he pulled out as it swung through the air and came down, slicing Mrs. Renaud's shoulder. Then, as quickly and he'd cut her, he was dragging her back to the sofa. Letting her up once more, he again he met her at the door, but this time the blade met her thigh. He made a sick game of his torture, allowing this to happen over and over until she'd sustained so many wounds that she begged for him to kill her.

"Please, just don't hurt my Reign," she pleaded, now pale and barely able to talk.

Those were her final words. After toying with her for nearly an hour, the bastard finally ended it.

"I'd never make a promise that I didn't intend on keeping."

That was the last thing Reign heard before the vision ended. When she was finally released, she collapsed to the floor sobbing.

"It's all my fault," she whispered. "You're dead because of me."

Chapter 19

When Reign was able to compose herself, she got up and headed back to her house. She was full of so many emotions, but rage trumped them all. There had to be a way to find out who this psychopath was, and when she did, he'd pay dearly. But there wasn't much for her to go on.

Without turning on a single light, Reign went to her room and retrieved the dagger she'd recently purchased and its thigh holster. There was no way that out of a city of nearly four hundred thousand people, no one knew anything. *Somebody* saw *something*; she'd just have to find out whom.

Turning to look into the mirror in the dim lighting, Reign didn't recognize the person staring back at her. What she planned on doing and how she was going to do it eluded her, but something had to be done. Taking a deep breath, she turned to walk out the room and was startled when she came face to face with her grandfather.

"Mô shæ, what are you doing?"

Reign stood there in shock staring at him. Months had gone by since her Paw Paw had passed. She'd called out to him many times begging to see him, but he never revealed himself.

"I've been calling for you," she said, tears streaming down her face.

"Wi, I know," he answered.

"So, you just chose to ignore me?

"Ou pa fô."

"No, English! And what do you mean I wasn't strong...of course I wasn't strong! What I was was broken! Mo té brizurye!" Reign screamed, tears streaming down her face.

Having every intention of simply walking through her grandfather's apparition, Reign began to head out of her room. But when she crossed into him she was met with another vision, and this time everything was crystal clear.

There were voices talking, and there was one she could recognize as her grandfather. People were moving about, but she couldn't change her focus. Her view looked like a picture frame, and Reign attention was intently set on the tea mug that's she'd given him so many years ago. She was becoming frustrated at not being able to see anything other than the stupid mug, but then something happened. A hand came into the frame with a small syringe and its contents were ejected into the tea mug. A few moments later her grandfather came smiling, picked up the mug and took a sip.

Reign knew what was to happen next, and she didn't want to see it. She fought desperately to pull herself from the vision but it would not let her go. So, standing there, she was helplessly trapped as she witnessed William Peyreux suddenly drop to the floor. It had only taken a matter of seconds before he had taken his last breath.

"Someone killed you," Reign said as her vision began to clear, but her grandfather was gone.

Walking slowly to her bed, she sat down. Tonight was turning into more than she had bargained for, and everything was taking a toll on her. There were so many images Reign would never be able to shake from her mind. She had already been subjected to witnessing the deaths of her mother and grandmother. And now Hania-Kele, Tempest, C.J., Mrs. Renaud and William had been added to the list. Her gifts were beginning to seem more and more like a curse.

"Paw Paw, I'm sorry for getting so angry," Reign said aloud, "but if your plan was to stop me…it backfired. I know you didn't want me to see what happened, but I did, and I'll never be able to get that image out of my head. Now I want this bastard more than ever."

Reign gathered herself and stood up. Leaving the room, she then headed out the front door and into the late-night air. She was angry, and nothing short of death was going to stop her from getting retribution for so much loss of life. Reign was finally realizing her potential, and that knowledge was extremely dangerous to anyone she considered a threat.

"I told you not to go to her," Amarrè said, chastising her husband as she watched her granddaughter walk out the door.

William sighed deeply and shook his head. "I had to try to stop her. She's not ready and she'll get herself killed. But this time they'll be no coming back."

"I pray to God that He disagrees with you," Amarrè said, right before they faded into nothingness.

The night air was balmy and the streets were noisy as Reign crossed over St. Louis Street. She didn't know what to look for, if she'd be satisfied with whatever was found or how ready she was to handle whatever might come her way.

"Hey baby!" a passerby called out.

Reign flipped her hood over her head. Being rude and a jerk weren't grounds enough to unleash her rage upon him, so she kept walking. Her objective was to be invisible, but if she happened to be seen, she didn't want to be memorable.

It had been a while since she'd gone out on a Tuesday night, so it was surprising to see just how many people flooded the streets. It wasn't too late, only about nine thirty, but everyone that walked passed her reeked of alcohol.

By the time Reign crossed Bienville Street she was very frustrated. So she stopped walking, stood still amid the busy sidewalk and listened. One thing that she'd started relying on with the growth of her gifts was her ability to hear and separate sounds.

Reign had been standing there for nearly ten minutes when she heard a familiar voice. Once able to separate it from the crowed, she remained still and listening intently.

"Yeah, I'm sure it's her. She's been standing there looking out of it for a few minutes. Maybe now would be a good time to grab her. No one would notice."

Whoever it was, he was definitely talking on the phone, but with all the commotion going on around her, Reign was having a difficult time making out the voice on the other end. Were they really going to make it this easy for her? Because if this was the best plan they could come up with, she wasn't going to stop them.

"Okay boss. I'll let you know when we got her," the voice continued.

Reign did not move an inch. She stood there, completely still and seemingly oblivious to her would-be abductors. Then, out of nowhere, she heard a terrified scream. However, it was far away enough that no one around her heard it, so no one reacted.

"No, please! What do you want? I have money, I can give you money," a terrified female voice screamed.

No, no, no Reign thought to herself. *I can't help you, I'm trying to fix my own problems.*

"Shuddup," the attacker commanded . "Move, make a sound and I'll slit your throat ear to ear. And it would be a shame to harm such a pretty little face."

The slurred speech and words of the attacker caused Reign to go cold. It was him, the same drunken imbecile that assaulted her a week ago. Continuing to listen intently, Reign could hear the woman take a trembling breath, then a zipper followed by her scream. *He gets off from frightening his victim?*

She could sense her overly cocky abductors drawing nearer in, what they thought, was an inconspicuous manner. Reign didn't know if she'd ever get this opportunity again, but she only had a split-second to make a decision.

"Damnit!" she whispered right before turning back and running full speed down Conti.

Now, to her it felt like one fluid movement. But to the men who were stalking her like prey, it played out as if she'd disappeared right before their eyes. And as Reign continued to follow the cries of the young woman, she heard their final words.

"Where did she go? She was literally standing right here."

"We'll have to call the boss. He's gonna want to know about this."

Reign had run six blocks up Conti Street before she stopped. Listening very carefully, she was unable to hear anything from the woman she'd heard screaming.

"Please don't let me be too late," Reign said aloud, then stood quietly, listening for any sound.

Then she heard him again.

"See, it's not so bad," the drunken man said through grunts. "I'm sorry about the bruises to that pretty face of yours, but I told you not to scream."

"No," Reign said, then ran across an empty dirt lot and into a row of abandoned and shabby apartments.

The moment she burst through one of the doors that had been boarded up, Reign heard a muffled scream. Making her way toward the commotion, she could feel her anger rise.

How dare he continue to go around thinking he can keep terrorizing women and taking what he wanted!

By the time Reign had gotten to them, she could see the woman's face bruised and bloody. Her skirt had been ripped and hoisted above her waist and trails streamed down her face from where tears had fallen and dried.

"Bastard," Reign said aloud before lunging at the man.

Minutes later she was walking over to where the woman lay, unmoving and catatonic.

"Come on, let's get you out of here."

Chapter 20

 By the time Reign had gotten back home it was nearly two in the morning. She'd managed to get the young woman, whose name she found out was Lena, to the hospital without being noticed. The last thing she wanted was to be seen wearing what she was wearing with a retractable dagger strapped to her thigh. Questions were not something Reign needed at this point.

The first thing she did was peel the sweaty clothes from her skin and take the hottest shower imaginable. Reign was frustrated that the evening didn't go as planned, but it did feel good to save that woman. Unfortunately, she was also brimming with regret. Had she not hesitated, she may have been able to save Lena's virtue as well.

However, there was now a more pressing issue to be dealt with. The men who were after her were now aware that she was not *normal*. Reign's situation had just become complicated at best, and from here on out she needed to be extremely careful.

Stepping out of the shower Reign towel dried her hair and headed to the kitchen to heat up her leftover take out. Being extremely hungry on top of being agitated, she kept telling herself that the good done that night outweighed losing her first potential lead.

Just as Reign sat down and turned on the television, there was a knock at the door. Before getting up she double-checked the clock and saw that it was two forty-seven in the morning.

"Just a minute," she called out.

After quickly grabbing the dagger that had been tucked in a loose wooden slab of the kitchen floor, she made her way to the door. Reign hesitantly peeked through the sidelight, but was immediately relieved when she found it was Dominic on the other side. First sliding the dagger in her waistband, Reign then opened the door.

"Isn't it kind of late for house calls?" she asked once he'd entered the house.

"Where have you been all day?"

Reign was taken completely off guard by his abrupt questioning.

"Not that's it's any of your business, but the girls and I went dress shopping, then we met up with James, Adrian and Krystian for lunch," she answered, with a hint of mild irritation.

Dominic was standing face to face with Reign in the living room as he questioned her. He didn't seem too pleased with her answer, so he continued.

"After that?"

"Are you seriously interrogating me now about my day?" Reign snapped before walking away from him and sitting on the sofa.

He looked completely disheveled as he raked his hand through his hair.

"Please Reign, just humor me. Where did you go after lunch?"

She sighed and continued. "We were there late, until around six maybe. Then I came home to relax."

"And that's it?" he asked.

"Yes, now please tell me what's going on."

"Reign, do you remember that night I told you I was going to check on you occasionally just to make sure you were safe?"

"Yes."

"Well, I came by to check on you tonight, around nine. You weren't home when I got here, which under normal circumstances would have been all well and good. However, just as I was leaving I happened to see you. And you were coming out of Mrs. Renaud's house."

He'd seen her. Why hadn't she been more cautious and aware of her surroundings. But it was too late now. She could either tell him the truth or fabricate her way out of this mess. She looked defeated as she opted for the former.

"Look, Mrs. Renaud had given me a key years ago. I wanted to see if I could pick up on something that maybe the cops had missed, you know, with my gifts."

"Reign," Dominic began, "that was probably not the smartest thing for you to do. Who knows who could be watching that house."

He stopped pacing the living room floor and sat next to her on the sofa. Reign saw a real fear in his eyes that her reckless actions had caused. She wanted to comfort Dominic by reassuring him that she'd never do something so stupid again, but she couldn't.

"Is there something else you want to tell me?" he asked.

Oh God please no, she thought to herself. *Please don't let him know about my vigilante move tonight.*

"No, nothing. I came back home and went over what I'd seen. It was traumatic to say the least. Why do you ask?" Reign said, hoping she wasn't about to be caught in another lie.

"There was a call to the station tonight. A man, the same one that attacked you, was found dead in an abandoned apartment building."

Reign's face paled in genuine horror. She *killed* him? Because she was pretty sure she'd only banged him up a bit.

"He's dead? But I thought he was in jail."

"He was. Got bailed out yesterday and was awaiting his court date," Dominic answered her, keeping his face resting down in his hands.

Reign really wanted to change the subject. Just the thought that she may have killed someone made her sick to her stomach.

"Maybe he messed with the wrong person and his luck finally ran out."

"Yeah," Dominic said with a heavy sigh.

Reign was sure her genuine reaction was enough to make Dominic believe her. He could never know that she was the one that did this. He'd never look at her the same.

Finally lifting his head, Dominic focused back on her. He reached out to touch Reigns face, but was surprised when she jumped back.

"I'm not going to hurt you," he said. And she could tell her involuntary action had wounded him.

"But that's the thing. When you touch me, it does hurt."

Dominic stared at her wordlessly, but in obvious confusion.

Reign sighed. "I want you. I want you and I don't understand any of it. But I can't have you because I'm in love with Krystian; and I can't sacrifice what I love for what I want."

Dominic desired to tell her that everything pointed to them being together, and that it wasn't her wanting him that she was feeling. It *was* love. But he stopped himself before the words ever reached his mouth. If her love for him were to ever happen, it couldn't be coerced.

"I should probably go," he said, and started to stand up.

But before he had an opportunity to stand, she reached out to stop him.

"Reign, you can't have it both ways."

"I know. But...I feel things when I'm with you. Things I can't explain."

"And it's obvious that the things you feel aren't strong enough for you to want anything more than my friendship. So why does being without me seem to bother you so much."

"I don't know."

Dominic stood up and started walking to the door. He didn't know how much restraint she expected from him, but if they kept talking like they were and at that hour, he refused to be held accountable for his actions. And just as he made it to the front door Reign darted in front of him, blocking his exit.

"There's more to us than just this thing with Justine, right?" she asked, voice shaking.

"I'm not doing this," was his only reply before attempting to reach for the doorknob again.

Reign continued to stand there, refusing to let him leave. Everything in her screamed to make him stay. Then, without a second thought, Reign gave in to her impulses. She tiptoed up, wrapped her arms around his neck and kissed him deeply.

She didn't know how it had happened, but she was instantly in Dominic's arms and he was carrying her back to the sofa. Every part of her was on fire as he laid her down, but didn't allow their lips to part. His full weight was on her, her arms stayed locked around his neck and he was holding her as if his very life depended on it.

"What are you doing?" Dominic said, finally breaking their heat filled kiss.

She looked up at him, her eyes a mixture of pain, passion and confusion. Everything about this woman tied him in knots, but he knew that if he took advantage of this moment, it was almost sure to end in disaster.

"I want you. I want you like I've never wanted a thing or person in my life."

"You want me right now. You want this moment. But I want more than a moment with you."

Reign's eyes flew open. His words were so familiar, like they had been spoken to her before. Then came the flood of guilt.

"Krystian," she whispered.

"One day things will be clear and you will know, without a doubt, what it is you want. I can't take advantage of you like this. It wouldn't be fair to either of us."

"Are you upset?" Reign asked as she instinctively twisted the hair at the nape of his neck around her finger.

"No, but I may have to renege on my restraint if you keep doing that. A man can take but so much," he answered, then pushed himself up off her.

"Yeah, you really should probably go now, especially since we crossed that invisible line. If we kiss again…" Reign trailed off in her attempt to joke, but was deathly serious.

"Yeah, I'm scared to even look at you right now," Dominic said with a smile, as he made his way to the door for the second time that night.

"I'll see you," she called out once Dominic was out the door and headed to his car.

The minute he pulled off, Reign closed the door and leaned heavily on it. She was fully and guiltily aware that the reason Dominic wasn't still in her house and making love to her was because *he* stopped what was going on. He was the one that reminded her that she was in love with another man. He was also the reason that she didn't have to *explain* anything to Krystian. But yet and still, there was this part deep down that wondered…*what if?*

Reign slept fitfully, tossing and turning all through the remainder of the night. And for once, it wasn't Nicola, death omens or anything of the like that caused her so much unrest. It was her own mind that drove Reign deeper into an agitated sleep. There was so much pressure on her, so many things that she couldn't escape, no matter how bad she wanted to.

Then, after more than two hours with no rest, the sun began to creep over the horizon. Reign continued to lie in bed as she wondered what Krystian was doing. What would he think if he knew that she was now officially a vigilante, and even though she was full of remorse over the blood that was now on her hands, she had no intention of stopping.

Reign had given Lisa the day off, so she had no choice but to get out of bed and make her way to the gallery. But she knew she wouldn't be focused on work. How could she when her life was continuously in jeopardy?

Getting up, Reign opened her blinds to let in the early morning light. She had always been happy with her life and accomplishments. Maybe if she had maintained a reasonable relationship with her father and included him in her life instead of rejecting him, none of this would have ever happened. Her existence seemed to have no happy median.

Heading to the bathroom she tripped over something on the floor. It was the black bodysuit. Kneeling down, Reign picked it up. Running her hands over the fabric, she could feel where something had dried and stiffened the material. *Blood.*

If she hadn't considered it before, it was definitely in the forefront of her mind now. She was strong, *really really* strong. Reign had to not only become familiar with her abilities, but learn how to control them. And though she was remorseful for the act itself, Reign didn't feel too distressed over the man she killed. After all, there was no doubt in her mind that if she hadn't stopped him, he would've killed Lena. However, what if she came across someone with far less dirt on their hands? She couldn't give in to her rage every time someone broke the law. That's what cops were for. That's what men like Dominic were for.

Reign didn't like the direction her thoughts were heading as Dominic invaded her mind, so she walked to the laundry room and threw the blood encrusted bodysuit into the washing machine. Turning to head back in her room and start getting dressed, she almost walked through Tempest's waiting apparition.

"Hi niece," she said.

"Hi," Reign said hesitantly.

"I saw you last night."

"And?" Reign questioned, half expecting her aunt to tell her that all of her powers were going to be stripped as punishment.

"We don't approve," Tempest began, "but we do understand. He almost killed you, he was going to kill her. Your remorse and need to control that blind rage you went into, that is what makes you different. You let go of an opportunity to potentially have your retribution, and possibly exposed yourself, to save the life of another."

At Tempest's words, Reign broke down in tears. She hadn't cried since her grandfather died. And so, everything from then until now had built up inside of her. The love, the anger, the hurt, the confusion…it was all just one giant mass of emotion.

Tempest's form went from that of an incandescent figure void of any physical body, to a being of substance. She was moved by Reign's tears and wrapped her arms around her, hugging her tight. In her heart, Tempest wished she could take on Reign's burdens as her own. She would never have a normal life, and love was sure to be the biggest challenge of all for her niece.

"You carry the weight of the world on your shoulders. You can't let the shortcomings that are guaranteed to happen drag you down too. If you did that, you'd never be able to stand."

Reign breathed through the last of her tears. Tempest was right. She had to find a medium, some kind of way to deal with the pressures only she knew.

"Do you know why you are so special?" Tempest asked.

Not trusting herself to speak just yet, Reign shook her head no.

"You are an anomaly. The blood that runs through your veins is the accumulation of several mighty lines. That is why you can chant and command the spirits in multiple tongues; it is also why combining the languages is so powerful. You are actually speaking to your ancestors and their gifts when you call down legacy magic."

The morning light was now high in the sky as Reign walked over to the sofa and sat down. The more she understood, the more things made sense. Now she knew why Nicola wanted to end Claudette's bloodline and why she was so desperate to prevent Reign's birth. Even in death, Nicola was unstoppable; but if a mightier opponent was inevitable and she could take their magic, her power would then become limitless and inescapable. There would be no one to challenge Nicola.

Tempest looked at Reign and nodded her head, as if she knew everything Reign was thinking.

"You are on the right path. It will be hard, but you must not give up."

The flood of knowledge Reign received had drained her mentally, and she almost dreaded having to go to the gallery. And as much as she wanted to just focus on the matter at hand, she knew she needed put energy into her career as well to help give her balance.

"How will I…" Reign began, but when she looked up, Tempest was gone. "Never mind," she mumbled, rolling her eyes.

Pushing herself up off the sofa, Reign went on to continue getting ready for her day. For the first time she hoped for a slow day at work, because it was starting out to be a sweats and t-shirt kind of Wednesday.

Chapter 21

The next few day for Reign were a blur. She had a never-ending stream of meetings, sales and private parties to host. And when she wasn't meeting someone or hosting something, her time was spent either meditating or practicing control over her combat techniques. Even though ending *her* attacker hadn't caused Reign an enormous amount of grief, she knew that she could not resort to that level of violence again unnecessarily.

Saving Lena had changed Reign in ways she never could have imagined. Protecting people from the scum of her beautiful city felt remarkable and fulfilling. And while she kept searching for her grandfather and Mrs. Renaud's killer, the decision Reign made to continue to protect the people of New Orleans gave her purpose where she would have otherwise been lost. She just had to make sure to stay off the police, and Dominic's, radar.

Aside from her new heroine complex, Reign had been avoiding Krystian like a plague. Oddly, it wasn't the kiss with

Dominic that had her dodging him, it was the fear that maybe she *had* chosen right. Maybe Krystian was her soul mate, and that thought frightened her in every imaginable way. Reign had never committed herself to anyone, and as much as she wanted him, being a part of something bigger than herself was daunting.

So now, as Friday's moon hung full in the sky, Reign was anxious. The bag kicking, along with practicing to precisely control her jujutsu moves, did nothing but increase Reign's already mounting anticipation. This would be the first night going back out since her initial spontaneous rescue, and she was ready.

It was after nine when Reign exited her house. As she walked through the French Quarter and toward the crowds that were guaranteed to be lingering on Bourbon Street, she felt like something out of a comic book. Cloaked in all black, hood pulled over her head and dagger strapped to her thigh, Reign allowed herself to blend in; becoming practically invisible to everyone she walked past. She did nothing to draw attention to herself, but saw and heard everything.

Reign's first instinct was to listen for the voices of her would be abductors from the previous night. If there was any chance they'd still be looking for her and take the bait, she needed to know.

Finding the unoccupied wall of a nearby bar, Reign positioned herself there for more than twenty minutes, listening intently. Throngs of people walked and stumbled down Bourbon Street, paying no mind to the woman that stood there, silently eavesdropping on them all. But after another fifteen minutes of nothing, Reign decided to give up and began walking among the partygoers.

"No fish tonight," she mumbled.

Weaving through the crowds of people that continued to wander aimlessly, she then decided to open herself up to something a little less purposeful. And Reign walked the streets for nearly an hour before something finally caught her attention.

"Please don't hurt us," she heard a woman's voice tremble frighteningly.

Turning, Reign tried to focus on where the voice had come from.

"You can have everything. Here, take it. Just leave us alone," a male voice pleaded.

You can't be too late this time, he has a gun, Reign said to herself.

Even though she had no clue where the voices came from, she could still smell the gunpowder and hear the hesitant squeeze of a finger on the trigger of a gun. Reign was becoming very anxious that she wouldn't find them in time when she heard a voice speak to her.

"Trust your senses," it said, almost whispery.

No sooner had Reign relaxed than every voice around her became clear and distinct. Once that happened, she was able to tell in which direction she needed to go. The clearer the voices became the closer she knew she was. And in just a matter of minutes she found herself in an unlit alley. There, cloaked in a dark corner, Reign could see that the gunman had a frightened couple backed against a wall.

"I gave you everything man. Now please, let me and my wife go."

"I can't do that," the gunman responded, "can't leave any loose ends."

Reign could not only hear trembling in gunman's voice, but she could smell his sweaty palms and fear. *He's scared,* she thought to herself. *He doesn't want to kill them.*

No sooner did he begin to squeeze the trigger than Reign revealed herself and emerged from the dark corner.

"You don't want to do this," she said, seeming to materialize from the shadows and slowly walked toward him.

The gunman quickly turned, and as he did, the gun went off. Fast as lightening, Reign moved to the side, just barely missing the bullet. Remaining calm, she resumed her slow pace and continued walking toward him.

"No! Keep the gun on me," she said when he attempted to return his attention to the frightened couple.

"Who are you!? What do you want!?" he demanded.

He couldn't see Reign's face. What her hood hadn't masked, the cloak of night was doing a good job hiding.

"My name is Isis," Reign said, thinking quickly. She definitely didn't want anyone knowing her real name. "What's yours?"

"This ain't no meet and greet!" he said forcefully, becoming visibly agitated.

Reign knew she was strong enough to take him down if she needed to, but that wasn't tonight's goal. She hadn't spent days meditating and gaining control over her energy just to pummel this misguided guy. She was now about four feet away from him, but continued to slowly walk forward.

"Well, I told you my name, I only thought it fair that you did the same," Reign answered with a smile.

"Kevin! My name is Kevin," he said after a brief pause while continuing to point to gun at Reign.

"Kevin, we should really talk about this situation we've all found ourselves in," she declared, then focused on the beating of his heart, which was racing.

"Well *you* wouldn't have been in it if you didn't mind your own damn business," he countered, but with less force than before.

Reign stopped walking when her chest was to the barrel of the gun. She stared intently at Kevin, who appeared to be no more than fifteen, but had the build of a man in his twenties. His eyes and body language spoke differently than his mouth. There was no way this kid just went around robbing and shooting people; she was starting to doubt that he'd ever hurt a soul in his life.

"Well, this kind of *is* my business. By trade, if I see something bad happening or someone about to get hurt, it is my duty to intervene. And since I've been doing this I have begun to realize that the people who do bad things aren't always bad themselves, sometimes they're just desperate. Not only that, but they also have the power to determine what I do with, *or to,* them by their choices," Reign said, still smiling.

"What do you mean, what happens *to* them," Kevin asked.

Reign still stood with the barrel of the gun in her chest and was deathly calm when she looked down at it. Without any warning or hesitation, she took the gun out of Kevin's hand, flipped it, and pointed it at him. Now Reign witnessed a different kind of fear in his eyes as he stood, dumbfounded.

"You two can go," she said to the couple. Once they left, she continued talking, "I could have done that at any time, but I chose not to. Do you know why?"

Kevin simply shook his head no.

"Because I value life. I'm not here to scare, hurt or kill anyone. I just wanted you to make a better decision on your own. How old are you?"

"Fourteen," he answered, averting his eyes to the ground and becoming noticeably restless. She could tell he wanted to say something else, but hesitated.

"Make the right choice," she reiterated.

"Isis, right?" he asked, finally looking up at her.

Reign nodded, then waited for him to continue.

"She came to me in my dreams. Said that if I didn't do exactly as she said, she'd kill my family."

Kevin looked around as he spoke, as if to make sure no one saw or heard him.

"Who?" Reign asked, and lowered the gun.

"She had these crazy purple eyes, that's all I can remember."

An intense chill came over Reign. Had Nicola really been watching her all this time? Her home was warded, so the only way her blood-thirsty great-grandmother could get to her was when she left the house.

"Does the name Nicola ring a bell?"

His eyes grew large with fear as he shook his head in the affirmative. "Yes'm that was it. Nicola. She said she needed to keep you distracted."

"Distracted from what?" Reign asked, fear mounting.

"From one of the eight. That's all she said."

"Go home, now!" she yelled, stepping back into the shadows.

"No! What about my family? She's gonna go after my family now."

"They'll be fine. It's not *your* family she wants," she replied, retreating into the darkness.

Reign ran as fast as she could to Adrian and Krystian's condo. She had to reason that her father was safe. Not only was his house warded, but he had the knowledge and strength to fight off Nicola if it came to that.

Still in her bodysuit and tabi boots, Reign began furiously pounding on the front door.

"Krystian!" she yelled when no one answered.

Then she saw the foyer light come on after what felt like an eternity.

"Hey, what's going on? Are you okay?" Adrian asked once he'd opened the door.

"No, not even a little bit. Where's Krystian? Please tell me he's here," Reign pleaded frantically.

"No, he's not," Alexa said, popping her head in front of Adrian, visibly shaken from Reign's urgent beating on the door. "He left to meet you about an hour ago."

"But I haven't spoken to him all day," Reign replied, trying to brush off the foreboding feeling that immediately came over her.

"Okay, come in while we get dressed. We'll go find him together."

"No," Reign whispered while backing out of the doorway, "just meet me at my house as fast as you can. I don't know how much time we have." And just like that Reign was gone.

Even though she ran to her house as fast as her legs would carry her, Reign somehow knew she was too late. And upon reaching her front door, her worst fears were confirmed.

"No," she said softly as tears began to roll down her face.

Reign must've stood there, motionless and helpless, for at least fifteen minutes before Alexa and Adrian showed up.

"What's wrong?" Alexa asked breathlessly, taking notice of Reign's tear stained face.

"Something is wrong," Reign answered, still staring at the front door.

"How can you tell?" Adrian asked.

"The blood," she said, walking to the door. "Someone tried to wipe it clean, but *I* can still see it."

Once Reign reached the entrance, she outstretched her hand and touched high up on the door.

"This is where he hit his head."

When Reign felt the spot, she was immediately enveloped in darkness. After a minute she could see Krystian walking up to her doorway, one lavender rose in hand and a captivating smile on his face.

Reaching the door, he rang the bell once, then twice. When there was still no answer he called out.

"Reign!"

"She's not here," a voice said from behind Krystian.

Taken by surprise, he turned to address the person. Reign could see from his expression that Krystian seemed to recognize the individual; but to her, whoever it was remained an obscure shadow.

"What are you doing here?" he asked impatiently.

"She said you'd be here. You're too predictable for your own good," the voice said with a bit of disdain.

"Who said I'd be here?" Krystian asked.

Reign could see a change in his eyes, which were no longer carefree and in anticipation of seeing her. They had become very wary and caution-filled.

"Well, since the Princess will no doubt be seeing all of this, I may as well kill two birds with one stone," the voice began. "Your girlfriend has become quite powerful. In fact, she is so powerful that you now have a very *necessary* contribution to make."

"I don't know what you're talking about," Krystian lied. "And what does Reign have to do with you anyway?"

"Do you really think my showing up was coincidental? You should know me better than that."

Reign heard the cocking of a gun. The gleaning metal of the barrel was placed against Krystian's forehead, but he did not flinch.

"You've never been one for a fair fight. Always hiding behind guns, or whatever else you could get your hands on,"

Krystian said, with a sneer of contempt. "You underestimate just how much Reign means to me if you think I'm going to let you harm one hair on her head. I was a fool for ever thinking I could trust you."

There was a moment where everything went eerily silent. Then the other voice continued, disregarding Krystian with a humorless laugh.

"You *will* to come with me now, or I'll just wait here until our gifted little magic maker shows up…because eventually, she *will* show up. And I'd hate for her to cross paths with a bullet that was meant for you."

Then suddenly, Krystian knocked the gun away and Reign could hear the connection his fist made with the would-be attacker's face. There was a moment where Krystian slammed the faceless figure to the ground, then threw several successful punches.

His win was short lived though, as two men came out of nowhere, rushed Krystian, then slammed him into the door. His head banged against it so hard that a small smear of blood was left behind.

When the man pushed himself off the ground his face entered the light for a split second. A trail of blood oozed from his lip and his eye was already turning blue from having received multiple punches. Then without warning, and while being pinned to the door by the two enormous men, Krystian received several blows to the face and gut.

"You won't get away with this," he said through clenched teeth.

"Does the name Nicola sound familiar?" the attacker continued with disregard.

Krystian looked up in shock and horror.

"I see it does. So you must know that, not only will I get away with this, but I'm going to enjoy every second. Maybe I'll keep you alive until your girlfriend comes for you; I suppose I could give her the courtesy being witness to your dying breath."

Then Reign was abruptly released from the vision. Shaking and crying she collapsed into Adrian's waiting arms.

"What did you see?" he asked.

"They have him," she answered.

"Who has who?" Alexa asked, kneeling beside Adrian and Reign on the ground.

"It's Krystian," Reign cried while Adrian continued to hold her. "Nathan and Nicola have Krystian."

www.ingramcontent.com/pod-product-compliance
Lightning Source LLC
Chambersburg PA
CBHW030657260626
47157CB00007B/2687